HOW MANY THERAPISTS
DOES IT TAKE?

How Many Therapists Does It Take?

The Wit and Wisdom of Psychotherapy

COMPILED BY

KENNETH E. REID

SEABOARD PRESS

JAMES A. ROCK & COMPANY, PUBLISHERS

How Many Therapists Does It Take?: The Wit and Wisdom of Psychotherapy
compiled by Kenneth E. Reid

SEABOARD PRESS

is an imprint of JAMES A. ROCK & CO., PUBLISHERS

How Many Therapists Does It Take?: The Wit and Wisdom of Psychotherapy
copyright ©2012 by Kenneth E. Reid

Illustrations by Carol Hannum

Special contents of this edition copyright ©2012 by Seaboard Press

Address comments and inquiries to:
SEABOARD PRESS
900 South Irby Street, #508
Florence, SC 29501
E-mail:
jrock@rockpublishing.com   lrock@rockpublishing.com
Internet URL: www.rockpublishing.com

Trade Paperback ISBN: 978-1-59663-735-1

Library of Congress Control Number: 2008939897

Printed in the United States of America

First Edition: 2012

For Dad...

For Elise and Reid

*With the hope I can pass on the kindness
and laughter he gave me.*

Laughter is a tranquilizer with side effects.

—Attributed to Arnold Glasow

Contents

A Note to the Reader

How many therapists does it take to change a light bulb? Answer—only one but it takes a long time—and the light bulb really has to want to change. All my professional life I have loved jokes about therapists and psychotherapy. For me they typically lighten the atmosphere, tickle the funny bone, help emphasize a point and ridicule the self-important. But, therapy jokes also do something extra—they echo back the absurdity and incongruity of our day-to-day lives.

I began collecting jokes and funny anecdotes about therapists—many included in this book—in the 1960's while a graduate student in social work. Funny stories, jokes, puns, quips, word play, and urban legends came from old joke books, cartoons, late night talk television, and more recently, the internet. Others came from my professors, fellow clinicians, and patients in the hospital where I trained. Interestingly, the jokes told by professionals were often the same ones told by the patients.

This genre of humor called *psychiatrist jokes*, with the stock caricature of the mad psychiatrist—a bald, bearded, Viennese analyst, who himself needed a psychiatrist—was inadvertently set in motion by Sigmund Freud and his followers in the 1930's. Added to the mix were stereotypes of the confusing mental hospital that made patients crazy, and the laughable behavior of highly resourceful patients.

Over time, *psychiatrist jokes* gave way to *therapist jokes* reflecting the growing number of helping professionals—psychologists, clinical social workers, nurses and counselors—practicing psychotherapy. Characterized by folly and exaggeration, *therapist jokes* have come to provide a fractured mirror reflecting the human condition—and the light-hearted funny side of life.

The collection of humor in this book is about the psychotherapeutic industrial-complex so enmeshed in American culture. These are the stories and jokes therapists tell each other during team meetings or over a beer after a long day. They are about stereotypes of therapists in ludicrous situations; folks facing outrageous predicaments of daily living; and overwhelmed hospitals and clinics confusing staff and patients alike. In short, the book is about the irony, folly, madness, and the outright comedy that undergirds the mental health establishment.

In spite of my affection for *therapist jokes*, certain humor, over the years, admittedly made me squirm. These were the rampant politically incorrect jokes that portrayed clients as excessively silly or ridiculous in their struggles with mind-challenging situations. Did this humor, I wondered, minimize the seriousness of emotional problems and contribute to the embarrassing stigma of mental illness—the stigma that psychotherapists, such as myself seek to erase.

With a measure of distance and emboldened by maturity, I have come to understand that the clients and patients in this humor bear little resemblance to actual individuals. Rather, these *therapist jokes* are about parodies, stereotypes, and caricatures of what we imagine therapists, patients, hospitals, and psychotherapy to be. They are not about *those* people, the *they'ns*, but rather about ourselves, the *we'ns*, revealing laughable qualities we would prefer to keep hidden. Freud had it right when he said that therapist and patient are inextricably connected, both sharing the same dis-ease.

To laugh at ourselves and the world around us is truly a gift. It is in this spirit that this volume was compiled.

A final thought. As much as I lampoon and poke fun at this phenomenon called psychotherapy and its mixture of wisdom and folly, effectiveness and ineptitude, I believe it to be a highly honorable and noble enterprise. Furthermore, I have special admiration for the courageous individuals and families who enter counseling to deal with the challenges of daily life. In spite of its quirks, millions of people each year are empowered to develop autonomy and independence and to live more functional lives.

My appreciation to a number of people who provided me with ideas and thoughtful criticism. These include Pat Kellogg, Robert Yesner, Havala McCall, Brian Beauchamp, Linda Rizzolo, and the Rt. Rev. Edward L. Lee. Appreciation also goes to my editor, Lynne Rock, for her sharp eye and helpful guidance. Gratitude goes to my wife Eve Reid, who not only read the early drafts but patiently listened to my telling many of the stories and jokes during parties and family get-togethers. Finally, special thanks to Carol Hannum for her delightful illustrations.

Kenneth E. Reid, Ph.D.
Kalamazoo, Michigan

Psy-cho-ther-a-py n. **1.** The care of the id by the odd.
2. The study of what people are up to that they should be
ashamed of. **3.** The process that enables us to correct our
faults by confessing our parents' shortcomings.

Psy-cho-ther-a-pist n. **1.** A mental detective. **2.** A person who
makes you squeal on yourself. **3.** A mind-sweeper. **4.** Someone
who will listen to you as long as you do not make sense.

Psy-cho-a-nal-y-sis n. **1.** The process in which a person spends
hundreds of dollar a session to talk to the ceiling. **2.** Confession without absolution. **3.** An approach that makes simple
people feel they are complex.

Chapter One

Don't Do As I Do:
Up Close and Personal

Psychotherapy is a spawning-ground of foolishness, pretentiousness and paradox—in other words, the very kind of human endeavor that humor was born to feed on.
—Harvey Mindess (1976)

It's hard to find a single stereotype of a psychotherapist. Some folks view them as paragons of mental health—well balanced, terrific parents, perfect spouses, and fountains of wisdom. Others characterize them as a bit crazy—out of touch with reality, and having more problems than those they seek to help.

The truth of course lies some place in between. Therapists are normal, flawed human beings who have no dispensation from complicated and embarrassing life predicaments. They, too, get angry at their children's behavior, divorce spouses, forget to pay bills, and feel hurt when family members forget to send them a birthday card.

The following jokes are about the personal struggles therapists face inside and outside the office, and underscore the old adage—*do as I say, not as I do.*

* * *

One thing therapists working together have in common is that they seldom agree. A psychiatrist, a social worker and a psychologist were walking in the woods when they spotted a set of tracks. The psychiatrist, with conviction, says," Hey, deer tracks!" The social worker, with confidence, says, "No, dog tracks!" The psychologist, with certainty, says "You're both crazy-they're cow tracks!"

They were still arguing when the train hit them.

* * *

A doctor visits a colleague and finds him in a state of progressive hysteria, shouting in frenzy, "I can't stand it anymore; I have to see a psychiatrist."

"But you are a psychiatrist," says the friend. "I know," the doctor replies, "but I'm too expensive."

* * *

Two counselors meet at their 20th college reunion. One is well dressed, freshly shaven, smiling, and looks like he just graduated. The other counselor looks old, disheveled, worried, and withered.

The older-looking one asks, "What's your secret? Listening to other people's problems every day, all day long, for years on end, has made an old man of me."

The younger looking counselor replies, "Who listens?"

* * *

A man went to a therapist and revealed his life story, all the details about his childhood, love life, hobbies, etc. At length, the therapist said, "There doesn't seem to be anything wrong with you. You're as sane as I am."

"But," said the client, "It's these butterflies, I can't stand them. They are all over me," whereupon he began brushing himself off with his hand.

"For heaven sake," cried the therapist, "don't brush them off on to me."

* * *

Bob and Marlene had been social work colleagues for years. Through thick and thin, they had become personally and professionally inseparable. They were excellent psychotherapists and had extensive experience with severely disturbed clients.

As time passed, their discussions with each other progressed from the profane to the religious, speculating about the existence of the afterlife. They promised each other that the one who died first would come back to tell the other if there was an afterlife; and, if so, whether they could practice psychotherapy in Heaven.

Bob passed away first; and after some time had elapsed, Marlene was well along in coping with her grief over his loss.

Imagine Marlene's surprise when Bob appeared to her early one morning. "Tell me," she cried, "is there an afterlife? And is psychotherapy practiced in heaven?" Bob responded, "I have good news, good news, and bad news."

"First, the good news. There is an afterlife!" he said. "Next, the other good news. Psychotherapy is indeed practiced in heaven."

"The bad news is that you see your first clients in an hour!"

* * *

A psychiatrist made it his regular habit to stop off at a bar on his way home for a hazelnut daiquiri. The bartender knew of his habit and would always have the drink waiting at precisely 5:03 p.m.

One afternoon, as the end of the workday approached, the bartender was distressed to find that he was out of hazelnut extract. Thinking quickly, he threw together a daiquiri made with hickory nuts and set it on the bar.

The doctor came in at his regular time, took one sip of the drink, and exclaimed, "This isn't a hazelnut daiquiri!"

"No, I'm sorry," replied the chagrined bartender, "it's a hickory daiquiri doc."

* * *

A man was attacked and left bleeding in a ditch. Two social workers passed by, and one said to the other, "We must find the man who did this. He needs help."

* * *

A most rude American psychologist wandered into a rathskeller in Munich and demanded a dry martini. The German waiter looked blank, so the psychologist repeated louder, "DRY MARTINI!"

The waiter shuffled off and came back with three martinis.

* * *

A priest, a rabbi, and a social worker were traveling on an airplane. Two engines caught fire. It was clear the plane was going to crash, and they would all be killed.

The priest began to pray and finger his rosary beads. The rabbi began to read the Torah. The social worker made use of the opportunity to organize a committee on air traffic safety.

* * *

"I'm treating a patient with a split personality," said a therapist, "and Medicare is paying for both of them."

* * *

A psychologist is at a party talking with a small group of people, when a man comes up behind him and taps him on the shoulder. The psychologist turns around, and the man hauls off and decks him.

The psychologist gets up, brushes himself off, turns to the group, and declares, "That's his problem."

* * *

Three social workers were sitting in the waiting room outside the pearly gates when St. Peter calls the first one up to the desk.

"So, what have you done to deserve to come here?" asked St Peter.

"Well," said the social worker, "I was a psychiatric social worker on the admissions unit of a state hospital. I worked many long hours under stressful conditions and helped to save many lives."

"Well, come right in and make yourself comfortable," St. Peter replied.

When asked what she had done to deserve to walk the streets of gold, the second social worker replied, "Well, I was a back ward psychiatric social worker during my lifetime. I worked many long hours and helped the team save many lives."

"Well, come right in and make yourself at home," replied Saint Peter.

"Now, tell me what you have done to deserve to sing with the angels?" he asked the third social worker.

"Well, I worked for a managed health care corporation during my lifetime. I worked many long hours under stressful conditions, and I helped to save the insurance company a lot of money," she beamed.

St. Peter looked puzzled for a moment, and then said, "Well, come right in and make yourself at home ... but you can only stay for three days."

* * *

A psychologist returned from a conference in Aspen, Colorado, where all the psychologists were permitted to ski for free. As she was unpacking, her husband asked, "How was the skiing?"

"Fine," she replied, "but I've never seen so many Freudians slip."

* * *

A man has a heart attack and is brought to the hospital ER. The doctor tells him that he will not live unless he has a heart transplant right away.

Another doctor runs into the room and says, "You're in luck. Two hearts just became available, so you will get to choose which one you want. One belongs to an attorney and other to a social worker."

The man quickly responds, "The attorney's."

The doctor says, "Wait! Don't you want to know a little about them before you make your decision?"

The man says, "I already know enough. We all know that social workers are bleeding hearts, and the attorney probably never used his. So, I'll take the attorney's!"

* * *

A psychologist was walking along a Hawaiian beach when he kicked a bottle poking up through the sand. Opening it, he was astonished to see a cloud of smoke and a genie smiling at him.

"For your kindness," the genie said, "I will grant you one wish!" The psychologist paused, laughed, and replied, "I've always wanted a road from Hawaii to California."

The genie grimaced, thought for a few minutes, and said, "Listen, I'm sorry, but I can't do that! Think of all the pilings needed to hold up the highway and how long they would have to be to reach the bottom of the ocean. Think of all that pavement. That's too much to ask."

"OK," says the psychologist, not wanting to be unreasonable. "I'm a psychologist. Make me understand my borderline patients. What makes them laugh and cry, why they are temperamental, why they are so difficult to get along with, what do they really want? Basically, teach me to understand what makes them tick!"

The genie paused, and then sighed, "Did you want two lanes or four?"

* * *

Two doctors opened an office in a small town and put up a sign reading "Dr. Smith and Dr. Jones, Psychiatry and Proctology."

The town's fathers were not too happy with the sign, so the doctors changed it to "Hysterias and Posteriors."

This was not acceptable either, so they tried "Schizoids and Hemorrhoids." No go.

Next they tried "Catatonics and High Colonics." Again, thumbs down.

Another attempt, "Manic-Depressives and Anal-Retentives." Still not good.

Further attempts—"Minds and Behinds" and "Lost Souls and Ass-holes." Nope.

"Analysis and Anal Cysts," "Queers and Rears," "Freaks and Cheeks," and "Loons and Moons." No takers.

Finally they found the solution to a perfect sign board: "Dr. Smith and Dr. Jones, Odds and Ends."

* * *

One behaviorist to another after lovemaking:

"Darling, that was wonderful for you. How was it for me?"

* * *

A psychotherapist had a roaring practice that he had started from scratch. Business was so good that he could now afford to have a proper sign created to advertise his wares.

He asked a young man to paint a sign board for him and put it above the entrance to his office.

But, instead of his business building up, it began to slacken. Women especially seemed to shy away from his practice, especially after reading the sign board.

"Maybe I have to rethink that sign," he said.

When he looked at the sign again, he understood the reason for the problem. The boy had found a small wooden board, so he had split the word into the three words:

Psycho-
the-
rapist

* * *

There was a psychologist who took a personality test and was most relieved to find he had none.

* * *

A lonely divorced counselor was driving home from work one evening when she saw a man trying to hitch a ride. She picked him up and they got to talking. "What do you do?" she asked him.

Embarrassed, he replied, "I recently escaped from the prison unit of a mental hospital."

"And why were you in a mental hospital?" she inquired.

"I was serving a life sentence for killing my wife," said the man.

Then the final question, "Oh, does that mean you're available?"

* * *

A Jesuit psychiatrist, a holistic therapist, and a clinical social worker were caught up in a political demonstration in a hostile Caribbean Island nation, once a colonial possession of France. In recent years, the island had been run by a cruel, anti-American dictator. The three persons were sentenced to death by the guillotine.

The Jesuit psychiatrist was chosen to be beheaded first. He asked that he lie face up, so that he could look to the heavens and to God when he was beheaded. The executioner raised the blade as high as it went then let it go. The blade stopped a few inches from his neck. The dictator's guards believed that this was an omen from God and let the psychiatrist go.

The holistic therapist asked that he be beheaded face down so that he could experience mother earth and see, at his last breath, the source of all his healing remedies. The executioner raised the blade as high as it went and then let it go. The blade stopped a few inches from his neck. The dictator's guards believed that this was an omen from mother earth and let the therapist go.

When it came time for the clinical social worker to be beheaded, he said to the executioner, "I believe that I can help you with the problem of that dysfunctional blade—use a little oil, and don't pull the blade all the way to the top! I'm sure it will work better that way."

* * *

Conversation overheard at a cocktail party:

"Are you a psychologist?"

"Why do you ask?"

"You're a psychologist."

* * *

Did you hear about the psychiatric chiropractor?

He specializes in attitude adjustments.

* * *

An annoying, self-righteous psychiatric nurse went to her general practitioner for a checkup. She said, "I feel terrible. Please examine me and tell me what's wrong with me."

"Let me begin with a few questions," said the doctor. "Do you drink much?"

"Alcohol?" said the nurse. "I'm a teetotaler, never touch a drop."

"How about smoking?" asked the doctor.

"Never," replied the nurse. Then she added, "Tobacco is bad, and I have strong principles against it."

"Well, uh," asked the doctor, "do you have much sex life?"

"Oh, no," said the nurse. "Sex is a sin. I'm in bed by 10:30 every night—by myself."

The doctor paused, looked at the woman hard, and asked, "Well, do you have pains in your head?"

"Yes," said the nurse, "I have terrible pains in my head."

"O.K.," said the doctor. "That's your trouble. Your halo is on too tight."

* * *

What did one therapist say to another therapist after lunch?

"Well, back to the minds."

* * *

Friend: Do you talk to your wife after sexual intercourse?

Psychiatrist: Only if there's a telephone.

* * *

A Canadian psychologist is selling a video that teaches you how to test your dog's IQ.

Here's how it works: If you spend $12.99 for the video, your dog's smarter than you.

* * *

A psychiatrist was unusually scornful of a patient who got into a panic every time he heard thunder.

"It's absurd to get into a fright over thunder—a harmless manifestation of nature.

Get a hold of yourself the next time you hear it. Do what I do—I simply put my head under the pillow and close my eyes until the thunder passes away."

* * *

First young woman: Why did you break up with that psychiatrist you were dating?

Second young woman: Because every time I showed up late for a date, he accused me of having hidden hostilities. And when I showed up early, he accused me of having an anxiety complex. And when I was right on time, he said I was exhibiting compulsive behavior.

* * *

A clinical psychologist was on his way home from his office late at night when he was accosted by a robber who said, "Your money or your life." Putting on his most arrogant air, the psychologist responded, "If you can't make such a simple decision, you need professional help."

* * *

What is the difference between a psychiatrist, a psychologist, and a clinical social worker? About 30 dollars an hour.

* * *

A therapist had her office decorated with new furniture made of overwrought iron.

* * *

A psychiatrist out walking with his wife passed a vivacious young blond who hailed him in a most friendly manner. The doctor's wife eyed him narrowly, "Where," she asked, "Did you meet that woman, my dear?"

"Just a person I met professionally."

"Whose profession, yours or hers?"

✳ ✳ ✳

The classified ad said, "Wanted: CEO needs a one-armed consultant with social science or behavioral science degrees and five years of experience."

The man who won the job asked, "I understand most of the qualifications you wanted.

But, why the one-armed consultant?"

The CEO replied, "I have many consultants, and I'm tired of hearing with each recommendation the phrase, 'on the other hand.'"

✳ ✳ ✳

During the 1990s, airports had to beef up their security. One airport went so far as to hire psychiatrists as security guards, so they could evaluate the mental states of the waiting passengers.

On the first day, a psychiatrist arrested a fellow psychiatrist and two psychologists.

✳ ✳ ✳

Two men are in a hot air balloon, and they drift into a dense cloud bank and are stuck there for hours. Finally they emerge, and they look around, not having a clue where they are. Seeing a man in a garden down below them, they yell to him, "Hello, down there. Can you tell us where we are?"

The man replies, "You're in a hot air balloon."

The first man turns to his partner and comments, "Just our luck. He's a psychologist."

"Why do you say that?" asks his friend.

"Well, what he said was obviously true, but it didn't help us at all."

✳ ✳ ✳

A doctor was addressing a large number of psychologists attending a national conference on health and well-being.

"The food we put into our stomachs is enough to have killed most of us sitting here years ago. Red meat is awful. Soft drinks corrode your stomach lining. Chinese food is loaded with MSG. High fat diets can be disastrous, and none of us realizes the long-term harm caused by the germs in our drinking water."

"But there is one thing that is the most dangerous of all and we all have, or will, eat it. Can anyone here tell me what food it is that causes the most grief and suffering for years after eating it?"

After several seconds, an older psychologist in the front row raised his hand and said softly, "Wedding cake."

* * *

A most enterprising young therapist who specialized in counseling older clients had this slogan adorning his letterhead: "REMEMBER THE MANIA!"

* * *

What's the difference between God and a psychiatrist?

God doesn't think he's a psychiatrist.

* * *

A social worker working in the emergency room of a hospital asks a very dejected and depressed man, "Was it liquor that brought you here?"

"Nope," replied the depressed man, "you can't get any in here."

* * *

Ten Signs Psychotherapists are Approaching Burn-Out

10. Thinks of the peaceful park they like as "their private thera-peutic milieu" ...

9. Realizes that their floridly psychotic patient, who is picking invisible flowers out of mid-air is having more fun than they are ...

8. When given a small gift by a grateful client, who thinks they walk on water, results in then having to debrief their feelings of unworthiness with a colleague ...

7. When watching a re-run of the *Wizard of Oz,* starts to cat-egorize the types of delusions that Dorothy had ...

6. When visited by their best friend who has severe relationship troubles, tries to remember which cognitive behavior technique has the most empirical validity for treating this problem ...

5. Realizes they actually have no friends, they have all become just one big case load ...

4. When asked how they are doing by a co-worker replies, a bit "internally preoccupied" and "not able to interact with peers" today ...

3. When asked by their spouse to set the table, responds that to do it would be "counter-therapeutic to their current goals" ...

2. Tells their teenage daughter she is not going to start dating boys because the girl is "in denial," "lacks insight," and her "emotions are not congruent with her chronological age" ...

And the number one sign the therapist may be burning out ...

1. Packs for a trip to a large family holiday reunion and takes along the DSM, "just in case."

—*Storm King* (2007)

* * *

Four psychiatrists were attending an out of town conference. Sitting in the hotel lounge one night they each agreed that it could be pretty tiresome listening to other people's hang-ups all the time. Wouldn't it be nice if someone would listen to their problems for a change?

"OK," said one, "why don't we reveal our innermost feelings now, just between the four of us? I'll go first if you like. My big hang up is sex. I can't get enough of it, and I have to confess that I frequently seduce my female patients."

The second said, "My problem is money. I lead an extravagant lifestyle way beyond my means. To finance this, I regularly overcharge my patients."

The third said, "My trouble is drugs. I'm a pusher and I often get my patients to sell drugs for me."

The fourth said, "My problem is that, no matter how hard I try, I just can't keep a secret."

* * *

After many years of complaining about low pay and difficult working condition, a group of psychologist, psychiatrist, and social workers have come together to form a union. They are calling it the United Mind Workers.

* * *

A pipe broke in a psychiatrist's home and a plumber was called. The plumber arrived that afternoon, took out his tools and did plumber-type things. After an hour he handed the doctor a bill for four hundred dollars. The doctor was shocked. "I don't make that kind of money as a psychiatrist," he exclaimed. The plumber gently answered, "Neither did I when I was a psychiatrist."

* * *

Mrs. Cohen came home from her Sisterhood meeting at the synagogue. She was very excited and explained to her husband that the guest speaker at the meeting was a psychologist from a nearby town who was a wonderful hypnotist.

Mr. Cohen then mentioned that attendance was down at the Saturday services. Maybe they should hire the psychologist to bring in a crowd. He talked it over with the rabbi, who thought it was a terrific idea.

After lots of publicizing, the synagogue was filled for the Sabbath service. The psychologist first explained the history of hypnosis then withdrew a pocket watch. As the crowd observed, mesmerized, the psychologist began, "Vatch the vatch. Vatch the vatch. Vatch the vatch." The congregants carefully observed, their eyes following the sway of the watch. Then accidentally the watch fell out of his hand.

"Crap!" he exclaimed!

It took them three weeks to clean up the synagogue.

* * *

Therapist: Mrs. Smith, that last check you gave me came back.

Client: Then we're even. So did my depression.

＊＊＊

An eminent psychologist was called to testify at a trial. A severe no-nonsense professional, she sat down in the witness chair unaware that its rear legs were set precariously on the back of the raised platform.

"Will you state your name?" asked the district attorney.

Tilting back in her chair she started to answer but instead catapulted head-over-heel backward and landed in a stack of exhibits and recording equipment.

Everyone watched in stunned silence as she extricated herself, rearranged her disheveled dress and hair, and was reseated on the witness stand.

The glare she directed at onlookers dared anyone to so much as smirk.

"Well, doctor," continued the district attorney without changing expression, "we could start with an easier question."

Chapter Two

A Matter of Degrees: Lessons Learned

When we remember that we are all mad, the mysteries disappear and life stands explained.
—Mark Twain

Becoming a psychotherapist is no simple task. Fledgling therapists attend lots of classes, take endless examinations, and write what seems like never-ending papers. Just about the time they have come to feel completely inadequate, they are sent off to do an internship in a clinic, hospital, or agency and told to apply the knowledge they supposedly learned in the classroom. Unfortunately, the *interesting* people they get assigned seldom resemble the case examples studied in their textbooks.

As they struggle with self-discovery, some great and terrible truths become clear. The first truth is that the major difference between their clients and themselves is that they're under more stress than the clients. The second is that a big part of being sane is being a little crazy, an insight that will prove most reassuring in the years to come. And third— they should have listened to their father and gone into business.

The humor in this section is about those additional life lessons gained in and outside the classroom.

* * *

How many psychology professors does it to take to change a light bulb?

One, with two grad students; but they must get three papers out of it.

* * *

How many social work students does it take to change a light bulb?

Could you repeat the question, please?

* * *

How many graduate students does it take to change a light bulb?

Two and a professor to take the credit.

* * *

How many social scientists does it take to change a light bulb?

They do not change light bulbs. They search for the root cause as to why the last one went out.

* * *

"Miss Johnson," said the professor, "name the man who originated study into conditioned reflexes."

"Umm ...," came the response.

"Does the name Pavlov ring a bell?" asked the professor.

＊ ＊ ＊

Letter from a psychology major enrolled in a course on subliminal communication:

Dear Dad,

$chool i$ really great. I'm making lot$ of friend$ and $tudying very hard.

With all my $tuff, I $imply can't think of anything I need. $o, if you would like, you can ju$t $end me a card a$ I would love to hear from you.

Love,

Your $on

The reply came back:

Dear Son,

I kNOw that astroNOmy, ecoNOmics and oceaNOgraphy are eNOugh to keep even an hoNOr student busy. Do NOt forget the pursuit of kNOwledge is a NOble task, and you can never study eNOugh.

Love,

Dad

＊ ＊ ＊

Professor lecturing to students on human development:

"In working with adolescents, remember there are five basic senses, plus one primary one." He continued, "The basic senses are smell, sight, hearing, touch, and taste." Having said that, he moved on to lecture on another topic.

An alert student raised his hand. "Excuse me, but you forgot to mention the primary one."

"Oh," responded the professor, "that's the one every parent and every teacher knows. It's the adolescent's sense of entitlement."

＊ ＊ ＊

A professor of psychiatry called on a pharmacist.

Professor: Give me some prepared tablets of acetylsalicylic acid.

Pharmacist: Do you mean aspirin?

Professor: That's it. I can never remember the name.

✳ ✳ ✳

Overheard in a lecture to social work students on nonverbal behavior:

"You will not be able to judge the happiness of a married couple from nonverbal cues alone," said the professor. "There are couples who hold hands, because if they let go, they are afraid they'll kill each other."

✳ ✳ ✳

Two psychiatric nursing students overheard talking about their professor:

"He's got such a big ego that when he prays he says, 'Dear God, do you need anything?'"

✳ ✳ ✳

A very shy guy goes into a local watering hole frequented by college students and sees a beautiful woman sitting at the bar. After an hour of gathering up his courage, he finally goes over to her and asks, tentatively, "Umm, would you mind if I chatted with you for a while?" She responds by yelling at the top of her lungs, "No! I won't sleep with you tonight." Everyone in the bar is now staring at them. Naturally, the fellow is hopelessly and completely embarrassed, and he slinks back to the table.

After a few minutes, the woman walks over to him and apologizes. She smiles at him and says, "I'm sorry if I embarrassed you. You see, I'm a graduate student in psychology, and I'm studying how people respond to embarrassing situations."

He responds at the top of his lungs, "What do you mean $200?"

✳ ✳ ✳

Woman: What school of thought do you come from?

Psychologist: Well, I always say I'm Freudian, but I'm really Jung at heart.

✳ ✳ ✳

A bright young woman wavered before choosing her career in medicine:

"Should I become a psychiatrist or a proctologist?" she wondered.

She ultimately flipped a coin to see how it came up: heads or tails.

* * *

A young psychiatrist serving his residency in a large ill-equipped mental hospital fell madly in love with a beautiful blond nurse with a reputation of being a gold digger. He finally worked up his courage and proposed matrimony. She stalled for a time, telling him coyly, "Not yet, my love. But come around again when you know how to own your own mind business."

* * *

A group of aspiring psychiatrists attending their first class on emotional extremes:

"Just to establish some parameters," said the professor to the student from Arkansas, "What is the opposite of joy?"

"Sadness," said the student.

"And the opposite of depression?" he asked the young lady from Oklahoma.

"Elation," said she.

"And you, sir," he said to the young man from Texas, "How about the opposite of woe?"

The Texan replied, "Sir, I believe that would be giddy-up."

* * *

There was a psychology student, minoring in statistics, who, when driving his car, would always accelerate hard before coming to a junction. The closer he got the faster he would drive. He would then whizz straight through it, slowing down once on the other side. One day his girl friend, traveling with him, understandably unnerved by his driving style, asked him why he sped up when driving through a junction.

"Well, statistically speaking," replied the student, "you are far more likely to have an accident at a junction, so I make sure that I spend less time there."

* * *

A young therapist was telling a supervisor about his trouble in getting intelligent responses from his patients.

"Suppose you ask me some of the questions you ask your patients," the supervisor suggested.

"Well, my first questions is: What is it that wears a skirt and from whose lips come pleasure?"

"A Scot blowing bagpipes," the supervisor answered.

"Right," said the therapist. "Now, what is it that has smooth curves and at unexpected moments becomes uncontrollable?"

"Roger Clemens' pitching."

"Right! What do you think of when two arms slip around your shoulder?"

"Why, a football tackle," replied the supervisor.

"Right," said the young therapist. "All your answers are amazingly correct. But you'd be surprised at the silly answers I keep getting!"

* * *

What did the sign on Pavlov's laboratory door say?

Please knock. DON'T ring the bell!

* * *

The psychiatrist is doing his rounds at his hospital with a couple of students. They look in on one patient, and the psychiatrist says to his students, "Sometimes this fellow thinks he's a temptress in a Bizet opera. But today, as you can see from his goose stepping, he thinks he's the World War II head of the Luftwaffe. What condition do you think he is suffering from?"

The first students replies, "Is he a paranoid schizophrenic with a multiple personality disorder?"

The second student says, "No, surely he just doesn't know whether he's Carmen or Goering."

* * *

The two college juniors yawned, and one said, "What shall we do tonight?"

"Let's toss a coin to decide," replied the other. "If it's heads we will go to a movie. If it's tails we'll call on Rosie and Suzie; and if it stands on the edge, we'll study for the psychology examination."

* * *

An experimental psychologist was studying the behavior of frogs. He put a frog on a flat surface, shouted "Jump," and the frog jumped. The psychologist reached for his notebook and wrote: Frogs can jump.

Then the researcher removed one of the frog's legs and shouted "Jump." The frog jumped, and the psychologist wrote down: Frogs can jump with three legs.

Then the psychologist removed another leg and shouted "Jump." The frog jumped, and the psychologist wrote: Frogs can jump with two legs.

He then removed the third leg and shouted, "Jump." With difficulty, the frog jumped, and the psychologist wrote: Frogs can jump with one leg.

He removed the frog's one remaining leg and shouted, "Jump." The frog didn't move. The psychologist repeated the command. The frog did nothing. The scientist concluded in his notebook: Frogs when deprived of all legs become deaf.

* * *

A statistician can have his head in an oven and his feet in ice, and he will say that on the average he feels fine.

* * *

First Rat: I finally got that experimental psychologist trained.

Second Rat: How so?

First Rat: Every time I go through that maze and ring the bell, she gives me something to eat.

* * *

A Stanford medical research group advertized for participants in a study of obsessive-compulsive disorders. They were looking for therapy clients who had been diagnosed with this disorder. The response was gratifying in that they received 3000 responses in the first three days after the ad came out. Unfortunately, the responses were from the same person.

✳ ✳ ✳

An elder professor in a school of social work was advising a young instructor. "You will discover," he said, "that in nearly every class there will be a student eager to argue. Your first impulse will be to silence him but I advise you to think twice before doing so. He probably is the only one listening."

✳ ✳ ✳

Three young women attended a psychology course on professional ethics and values. The professor started by asking a question. "What would you do," he asked, "if you were on a small boat and saw a ship coming at you? On board were a thousand sex-crazed sailors. What would you do to avoid any problem?" One student said, "I'd turn my boat as fast as I could and try to get away."

A second said, "I'd hold my course and pray that my pistol would keep them away."

The third, who hadn't had a date in months, said, "What's the problem?"

✳ ✳ ✳

Senior psychiatrist: You seem to have cured the patient. What's worrying you now?

Third Year Resident: I filled him up with so many medicines, I don't know which one worked.

✳ ✳ ✳

A high school student wrote in a paper, "I would like to be a psychologist. I plan on taking as much psychology as possible in college and maybe someday emerge another Fraud."

✳ ✳ ✳

The psychology instructor had just finished a lecture on mental health and was giving an oral test on the various forms of psychopathology.

Speaking specifically about bipolar behavior, she asked, "How would you diagnose a patient who walks back and forth screaming at the top of his lungs one minute, then sits in a chair weeping uncontrollably the next?"

A young man in the second row raised his hand and answered, "A basketball coach?"

* * *

During a course on parapsychology, the professor was lecturing on the topic of ghosts and the occult.

"How many of you believe in ghosts?" asked the professor.

Approximately 50% of the class raised their hands.

"That's about the national average. And how many of you have seen ghosts?"

This time 10% of the students raised their hand.

"Again," said the professor, "that's the national average."

Deciding to have a little fun he asked, "And, how many of you have made love to a ghost?"

A rural looking lad wearing a John Deere cap, sitting in the last row, put his hand up.

The professor was shocked by the response. "That's quite unusual. Come down to the lectern and tell us your experience of making love to a ghost."

"Ghost," exclaimed the student, "I thought you said goat!"

* * *

A young male therapist whose caseload consisted primarily of women was troubled by the reality that he was sexually attracted to several of them. Feeling confused he brought up his concern with his much older and experienced supervisor. "I know it's just counter-transference," said the young man, "but when will I get over this problem?"

"Three days after you're dead," replied the older supervisor with an understanding smile.

* * *

A team of psychology professors from a well known Ivy League university received a grant to study the behavioral patterns of a certain group of bears living above the Arctic Circle. Inuit Eskimos in the region reported that the bears' behavior was in constant flux. One week the animals were excited, agitated and full of energy. The following week they were sad, depressed and fatigued.

After four years of study the psychologists diagnosed the reason for their unusual behavior. The bears were bipolar.

* * *

It was an advanced psychology course on human behavior and the professor, in her late sixties, was lecturing on the problems of premarital sex. "Our patients risk their future because of desire and sexual gratification."

"Would you," she asked, "risk your future for an hour of pleasure?"

One young student in the middle of the classroom raised her hand and asked, "How do you make it last an hour?"

* * *

Nursing Students—Final Examination

History: Describe the history of nursing from its origin to the present day, concentrating especially but not exclusively on its social, political, economic, religious and philosophical impact on Europe, Asia, America, and Africa. Be brief, yet specific.

Surgery: You have been provided with a razor blade, a piece of gauze, and a bottle of Scotch. Remove your appendix. Do not suture until your work has been inspected. You have 15 minutes.

Psychology: 2,500 riot-crazed aborigines are about to storm the classroom. Calm them using any coping mechanism you feel confident in using. Explain your reasoning.

Biology: Create life. Estimate the difference in subsequent human culture if this form of life had developed 500 million years earlier with special attention paid to its probable effect on the English parliamentary system. Prove your thesis.

Sociology: Estimate the sociological problems that might accompany the end of the world. Construct an experiment to test your theory.

Epistemology: Take a position for or against truth. Prove the validity of your position.

Philosophy: Sketch the development of human thought: estimate its significance. Compare it with the development of any other kind of thought.

Physics: Sketch the nature of matter. Include in your answer an evaluation of the impact of the development of the Band-Aid.

Political Science: There is a red telephone on your desk. Start World War III. Report at length on its socio-political effects, if any.

General Knowledge: Describe knowledge in detail. Be objective and specific. You have 15 minutes. (If you have any questions, raise your hand!)

—*Shirley J. Braverman* (June 1980)

* * *

A nurse in the maternity ward asked a young medical student why he was so enthusiastic about obstetrics. He said sheepishly, "When I was on medical rotation, I suffered from heart attacks, asthma and itch. In surgery, I was sure I had ulcers and pancreatitis. In psychiatry, I couldn't decide if I was psychotic or had multiple personalities. Now, in obstetrics I can relax."

* * *

After the college boy delivered a pizza to a trailer house, the man asked, "What's the usual tip?"

"This is my first trip here," replied the young man, "but the other guys say if I get a quarter out of you, I'll be lucky."

"Is that so? Well, just to show them how wrong they are, here are five dollars."

"Thanks," replied the student. "I'll put it to my college fund."

"What are you studying?" asked the man.

The lad smiled and said, "Applied psychology."

Chapter Three

Paralysis of Analysis: Getting to Know You

There is only one difference between a madman and me. I am not mad!
    —Salvador Dali (1952)

Who is disturbed and who is healthy? Who's insane and who is sane? Who needs counseling and who doesn't? Psychotherapists struggle with these questions every day. Early in their careers, therapists tend—un-wittingly—to separate people into two broad categories, the *"we' ens"*—those who are healthy—and the *"they'ens"*—those who are unhealthy. The differences between health and illness, for the young therapists, will never be this clear again.

As professionals mature, they begin to comprehend their own mad-ness and sanity. Mysteries disappear, and the behaviors once thought of as dysfunctional begin to make greater sense. That line—which once seemed so unambiguous, separating sanity and madness, and the *"we'ens"* and *"they'ns"*—becomes blurred. Is it no wonder that mental health has never been contagious, nor has there ever been a wellness epidemic.

The following humor illustrates the underrated fact that reality is the leading cause of stress.

✳ ✳ ✳

"I think I'm manic depressive!" said the client.

"Calm down, cheer up, calm down, cheer up ... " replied the therapist.

✳ ✳ ✳

Insanity is doing the same thing over and over again but expecting a different outcome.

—*Rita Mae Brown* (2006)

✳ ✳ ✳

When the new patient was settled comfortably in the chair, the counselor began the therapy session. "I'm not aware of your problem," the counselor said, "so perhaps you should start at the very beginning."

"Of course," replied the patient. "In the beginning, I created the Heavens and the Earth ..."

* * *

There is one advantage to being poor—a therapist will cure you faster.

* * *

"Doctor," the patient said, "my wife thinks I'm crazy because I like sausages."

"Nonsense!" said the doctor, "I like sausages, too."

"Good," responded the patient, "you should come and see my collection. I've got hundreds of them."

* * *

In most cases the difference between depression and disappointment is your level of commitment.

—*Marc Maron* (2009)

* * *

A man went into a therapist's office and sat in a plush chair. He took out a pouch of pipe tobacco and stuffed some in his ear. Watching this, the therapist said, "It seems you have come to the right place. How can I help you?"

The man replied, "You can give me a light."

* * *

The therapist told the patient that he was conducting a simple test to monitor normal human responses. "So," began the therapist, "what would happen if I cut off your left ear?"

"I wouldn't be able to hear," replied the patient.

"And what would happen if I cut off your right ear?"

"I wouldn't be able to see?" said the patient.

"Why do you say that?" asked the therapist.

"Because my hat would fall over my eyes," replied the patient.

* * *

Do you know the difference between a psychotic and a neurotic?

The psychotic thinks that two plus two is five. The neurotic knows that two plus two is four—but he *hates* it!

* * *

A man walked into the therapist office. He wore a purple shirt, a seventeenth-century cape and a Napoleon hat. On his feet were spurs that jangled, and tied around his waist was a braided silk rope which pulled a toy fire engine when he walked. In one hand he held a lollipop and in the other a jelly donut. "Doc," he said, "I come to talk to you about my brother."

* * *

Why did the Siamese twins go to a psychotherapist?

They were co-dependent.

* * *

My sister was diagnosed with multiple personalities. She called me the other day and my caller ID exploded.

—*Zack Galifanakis* (2009)

* * *

A man goes to a psychologist and says, "Doc, I got a real problem. I can't stop thinking about sex."

The psychologist says, "Well, let's see what we can find out," and pulls out his ink blots.

"What is this picture of?" he asks.

The man turns the picture upside down and then turns it around and states, "That's a man and a woman on a bed making love."

The psychologist says, "Very interesting," and shows the next picture.

"And what is this picture of?"

The man looks and turns it in different directions and says, "That's a man and a woman on a bed making love."

The psychologist tries again with the third ink blot, and asks the same question, "What is this picture of?"

The patient again turns it in all directions and replies, "That's a man and a woman on a bed making love."

The psychologist states, "Well, yes, you do seem to be obsessed with sex."

"Me?" demands the patient. "You're the one who keeps showing me the dirty pictures."

* * *

There was a social worker who discovered a simple assessment tool for determining whether a client was ready to leave an inpatient mental health facility. The client was asked to repeat a procedure: The social worker touched her wrist, elbow, and shoulder in that order and said, "Wrist, elbow, shoulder."

The first client tried it and said, "Wrist, shoulder, elbow" (touching elbow when saying shoulder).

The second client said, "Elbow, shoulder, wrist" (while touching wrist, elbow, shoulder).

The third client got it right with "Wrist, elbow, shoulder."

"That's great!" said the social worker. "How did you do it?"

The client pointed to his temple and said, "Kidneys."

* * *

A man goes to a psychiatrist and says, "Doc, I think I'm gay and it worries me."

The psychiatrist asks, "Why do you think you're gay?"

"Because my grandfather is gay."

"Well, just because your grandfather is gay doesn't mean you're gay."

"But my father is gay, too."

"Well, just because your grandfather is gay and your father is gay doesn't mean you're gay."

"But my brother is gay, too!"

The psychiatrist looks at him and says, "Isn't there anybody in your family who likes women?"

"Yeah, I think my sister does!"

* * *

I'm passive aggressive. That's what a counselor labeled me, which really ticked me off.

But, I couldn't do a thing about, not right then—but I made plans.
—*Milt Abel* (2009)

* * *

A young woman says to her therapist, "Doctor, is this normal? Every time my husband and I have intercourse, I feel very cold or very hot."

After a series of tests in which no cause is discovered, the doctor calls in the husband and asks his opinion about the phenomenon his wife has reported.

"It is quite simple," says the husband. "We only make love twice a year, once in the summer and once in the winter."

* * *

The man sitting in the therapist's office was complaining about an obsession that was ruining his life. "It's baseball, doctor," he said. "Please help me. Baseball is destroying me. I can't even get away from it in my sleep. As soon as I close my eyes, I'm out there chasing a fly ball or running around the bases. When I wake up, I'm more tired than I was when I went to bed. What am I going to do?"

The therapist sat back and folded her hands. "First of all," she said, "you have to make a conscious effort *not* to dream about baseball. For example, when you close our eyes try to imagine that you're at a party and someone is about to give you several million dollars."

"Are you crazy, doctor?" the patient roared. "I'll miss my turn at bat!"

* * *

The statistics on sanity are that one out of every four Americans is suffering from some form of mental illness. Think of your best three friends. If they're okay, then it's you.

—*Attributed to Rita Mae Brown*

* * *

Did you hear about the depressed proctologist? He's been feeling down in the dumps.

* * *

"Doctor," says the patient, "you must help me. I'm under such a lot of stress that I keep losing my temper with people."

The doctor replies, "Tell me about your problem."

The patient retorts, "I JUST DID DIDN'T I, YOU STUPID JERK!"

* * *

I tried to smother myself with a pillow. That doesn't work. I couldn't breathe.

—*Del Ray Davis* (2009)

* * *

A woman walks into a dentist's office.

"What can I do for you?" asks the dentist.

"I think I'm a moth," replies the woman.

"You don't need a dentist, you need a psychiatrist!" says the dentist.

"I know!" replies the patient.

"Well, why did you come in here then?" asks the dentist.

"The light was on ..."

* * *

An elderly woman goes to see a psychiatrist. "Doctor, my husband worries me. I'm afraid he is losing his potency. I'm wondering if the reasons are emotional or physical."

The psychiatrist, a bit surprised, thinks a moment and asks, "Could you tell me your age please?" "I'm 82," the woman replies.

The doctor reflects on her answer and smiles. "And what age is your husband?"

"He's 85," comes the reply.

This time the doctor looks confused. "When did you first discover he was impotent?"

"The first time was yesterday evening. But what really worries me is that it happened again this morning."

* * *

Did you hear about the psychotic with low self-esteem? He only wants to assassinate the Vice President.

—*Bob Nickman* (2009)

* * *

A middle-aged Texan went to a psychiatrist:

"Doc," he began, "I shore need yore help. I'm in a bad way. I been a Texan all my life and suddenly I just don't give a damn!"

* * *

"I'm a sick man. I'm dying from liver disease," said the new client.

"Impossible, you wouldn't be able to tell. With liver disease, there's no discomfort," replied the therapist.

"Right," said the client, "those are exactly my symptoms!"

* * *

I love Wal-Mart, it's my favorite store. I just go there when I'm depressed. You don't need Prozac. Just five minutes there and I'm saying to myself, "Damn, my life ain't that bad."

—*Steve McGrew* (2009)

* * *

A distraught man goes to see a psychologist:

"How may I help you?" the doctor asks.

"Well, Doc, every night, I have the same dream. I'm lying in bed and a dozen women walk in and try to rip my clothes off and have wild sex with me."

"And then what do you do?" the psychologist asks.

"I push them away," says the man.

"Then what do you want me to do to help you?"

"Break my arms!" says the man.

* * *

A woman runs into a stationery store and confronts the clerk, "Did you see me come in that door?" she asks breathlessly.

"Yes," says the confused clerk.

"Have you ever seen me before?" she asks.

"No, I haven't," the clerk replies.

"Then how did you know it was me?"

* * *

One nice thing about egotists: They don't talk about other people.

* * *

Therapist: Do you have trouble making up your mind?

Patient: Well, yes and no.

* * *

Client: "I tried to kill myself yesterday by taking a thousand aspirin."

Therapist: "What happened?"

Client: "Oh, after the first two, I felt better."

* * *

Neurotic means he is not as sensible as I am, and psychotic means he is even worse than my brother-in-law.

—*Attributed to Karl Menninger, M.D.* (2005)

* * *

"So," said the therapist, "You think you are a dog. How long have you been subject to this dangerous hallucination?"

"Ever since I was a puppy."

* * *

A fellow who thought he was a dog went to a therapist and immediately began long-term therapy. When it was all over, a friend asked him how he felt. He said, "Fine. Feel my nose."

* * *

The FDA approved a Prozac-type drug for dogs who are depressed. This is good because it is hard for dogs to get therapy, since they are never allowed on the couch.

—*Colin Quinn* (2009)

* * *

Client: I have a problem. I feel depressed and worthless.

Therapist: You should cut down on your drinking.

Client: I don't drink and have never touched a drop in my life.

Therapist: You should cut down on your womanizing.

Client: Good heavens! I haven't touched a woman in my entire life.

Therapist: Your problem is you have no problems! Get yourself a drink, learn to smoke, find a couple of girl friends, and you'll be all right.

* * *

After two years of intensive counseling, a therapist referred his client to a physician because of the man's complaints of terrible neck pain, throbbing headaches, and dizzy spells. The doctor examined him and said, "I regret to inform you that you have only six months to live."

The doomed man decided he would spend the time he had left enjoying himself. He took all of his money out of the bank and bought a car, a boat, and a plane. Then he went to get himself new clothes. The first thing he purchased was a dozen new custom-made shirts.

The tailor measured him and said, "You have a size 17 neck."

"Impossible," said the man. "I wear a size 15 and that's what I want."

"I'd be glad to do it for you, sir," said the tailor, "but, if you wear a size 15 neck, you'll probably have terrible neck pains, throbbing headaches, and dizzy spells."

* * *

A man walks into a psychiatrist's office:

"Doc, every time I see nickels, dimes and quarters I have a panic attack! What do you think my problem is?"

"Oh, that's easy," the doctor said. "You're just afraid of change."

* * *

A Selection of Christmas Carols for Your Dysfunctional Friends.

SCHIZOPHRENIA
Do You Hear What I Hear?

MULTIPLE PERSONALITY DISORDER
We Three Queens Disoriented Are

DEMENTIA
I Think I'll Be Home for Christmas

NARCISSISTIC
Hark the Herald Angels Sing about Me

MANIC
Deck the Halls and Walls and House and Lawn and Streets and Stores; and Office and Town and Cars and Busses and Trucks and Trees and Fire Hydrants and ...

PARANOID
Santa Claus is Coming to Get Me

PERSONALITY DISORDER
You Better Watch Out, I'm Gonna Cry, I'm Gonna Pout, Maybe I'll Tell You Why

DEPRESSION
Silent Anhedonia, Holy Anhedonia, All is Flat, All is Lonely

OBSESSIVE-COMPULSIVE DISORDER
Jingle Bell, Jingle Bell, Jingle Bell Rock

... (better start again),

Jingle Bell, Jingle Bell, Jingle Bell Rock

... (better start again),

PASSIVE-AGGRESSIVE PERSONALITY
On the First Day of Christmas, My True Love Gave to Me (and then took it all away)

BORDERLINE PERSONALITY DISORDER
Thoughts of Roasting on an Open Fire

* * *

"I was feeling a bit depressed the other day so I called the Suicide Help Hot Line. I was put through to a 'call center' in Pakistan. I explained that I was feeling suicidal.

They were very excited at this news and wanted to know if I could drive a truck."

* * *

Did you hear about the dyslexic, agnostic, insomniac? He stayed up all night wondering if there was a dog.

* * *

Patient: Doctor, you have to help me. Some mornings I wake up and think I'm Donald Duck, other mornings I wake up and think I'm Mickey Mouse.

Doctor: How long have you been having these Disney spells?

* * *

I went to the doctor and he said, 'You've got hypochondria.' I said, 'Not that as well!'

* * *

I don't know if you call it an inferiority complex but I've an exaggerated idea of my own unimportance.

* * *

Classified Ad:

Help wanted: Telepath, you know where to apply.

* * *

I have a very addictive personality. In fact, I just bought a book on addiction. I love it so much I can't put it down.

—*Scott Kennedy* (2009)

* * *

A woman went to her counselor insisting her skin was gold. The counselor diagnosed it as nothing serious, just a gilt complex.

* * *

Then there was the ego maniacal and narcissistic patient who was told by her doctor she was suffering from "I" strain.

* * *

According to research completed by a well known school of psychiatry, it is a proven fact that you can learn a lot about individuals suffering from paranoia by just following them around.

* * *

Masochist to sadist: Hurt me!

Sadist to masochist: No!

* * *

A junior officer at the Pentagon was a hard worker, and had a nice well-furnished office. However, he began behaving strangely. First he shoved his desk out into the space also occupied by his secretary's desk. Then a few days later, as he was leaving for the day, he pushed his desk into one of the many long corridors. He worked there for a few days, and then shoved his desk into the men's room and set up work there.

This unusual behavior did not escape the notice of his colleagues or his supervisor. Their discomfort with his behavior, however, prevented them from going to the officer directly. Instead, they went to the division psychiatrist and asked him to intervene.

So the psychiatrist walked into the men's room and asked, "Why have you kept moving your desk? More important, why have you moved it into the men's room?"

"Well," said the officer, "I figure that this is the only place in the Pentagon where they know what they are doing."

* * *

It was a bad night. I dreamed I was eating shredded wheat and woke up to find my mattress missing.

* * *

Neophyte nurse to patient: "You are an *acute psychotic*."

Patient: "Call me a cute psychotic again and I'll punch you!"

* * *

One fellow didn't know whether he really wanted to commit suicide, so he threw himself in front of a parked car.

* * *

A man checked into an Atlanta hotel. Going straight to his room, he forced open the window, got out on the ledge, and prepared to jump. A policeman rushed up and started to calm him. "Don't jump." said the policeman.

The man shook his head, "I have nothing to live for."

"What about your family? For your family's sake, don't jump."

"I have no family."

"Think of your friends. Don't jump."

"I have no friends."

"Then for the honor of the South and the spirit of Jefferson Davis, don't jump."

"Who's Jefferson Davis?"

"Jump, Yankee!"

* * *

It's great the way psychiatrists throw big words at you. I went to one and he told me, "I see you're suffering from Cashew-Maraschino Syndrome." I said, "What's that?" He said, "Nutty as a fruitcake."

* * *

The therapist, after an assessment, had come to the conclusion that the man's main problems were deceitfulness and self-delusion. "How do you make your living?" he asked.

"I built three million fabricated homes."

"THAT'S A LIE!" confronted the therapist.

"I told you it was fabricated."

* * *

Psychiatrist: I believe your depression is rooted in deep-seated feelings of hostility and inferiority, first manifested in childhood due to an overbearing mother and a rather docile father, but reinforced significantly by inhibited extroverted siblings and a rather crowded home life.

Patient: But doc...I'm not depressed.

Psychiatrist: So, I took a shot.

* * *

"Doctor," asked the patient, "even though you've diagnosed me as having a multiple personality, is it all right to get married?"

"Well," said the doctor, "who are you planning to marry?"

"The Johnson triplets."

* * *

Advice to a therapist when assessing whether a mathematician is an introvert or extrovert. "If he looks at your shoes, he's an extrovert."

* * *

A man goes to a therapist's office and says, "Doc, you have to help me! Every night I dream I'm a sports car. The other day I dreamed I was a Trans Am. Another night I dreamed I was an Alfa Romero. Last night I dreamed I was a Porsche. What does this mean?"

"Relax," says the doctor. "You're just having an auto body experience."

* * *

A fellow walks into a therapist's office with a concerned look on his face. "I'm having that dream again," he says.

"What dream?" asks the therapist, not really paying attention.

"You know," says the man, "the one where I'm into bestiality, sadism and necrophilia."

Now the therapist is listening.

"Should I be worried," he asks, "or am I just beating a dead horse?"

Chapter Four

Some of My Best Friends:
Politically-Correct Diagnoses

Right now I'm having amnesia and déjà vu *at the same time. I think I have forgotten this before.*
—Steven Wright (2009)

Regrettably, only 0.1 percent of the population has had training in the classification of questionable behaviors. Therapists spend countless hours attending courses on abnormal psychology, psychopathology, and social deviance. There they learn the magical language that provides the power to separate one person's behavior from another. Over time, this diagnostic labeling—referred to as psychobabble by the cynics—is incorporated into their everyday vocabulary. Phrased to resemble medical diagnosis, psychiatric labels such as obsessive-compulsive and dissociative reaction become old hat and easily dropped into conversation impressing friends, family, and strangers. The bad news is that no two therapists agree on a single definition of these terms.

So, here are some quick, easy, and politically-correct labels we can all use. Less stigmatizing, they are almost as precise and accurate as the ones taught to psychotherapists.

She has ...

a photographic memory, but the lens cap is on

only one oar in the water

bubbles in her think tank

an IQ of room temperature

a Teflon brain: nothing sticks

a leak in the skylight

She is …

all telephone, no receiver

swimming in the shallow end of the gene pool

not the quickest bunny in the forest

one wave short of a ship wreck

sharp as a pound of wet liver

driving on only three wheels

ten cents short of a dollar

not an idiot, but plays one in life

She is a …

shining example of why you should avoid inbreeding

legend in her own mind

medical mystery

poster child for birth control

pane short of a window

result of too much chlorine in the gene pool

button short of a shirt

He has …

taken one too many punches to the head

all his eggs in the same basket

donated his brain to science before he was done with it

a mind like a steel trap—rusty and illegal in 37 states

an IQ lower than his shoe size

diarrhea of the mouth and constipation of ideas

a parachute, but is missing the ripcord

delusions of adequacy

slates missing from the roof

He is ...

> *one tree short of a hammock*
>
> *all missile, no warhead*
>
> *dumber than a frozen mukluk*
>
> *dumber than a bag of hammers*
>
> *as popular as a French kiss at a family reunion*
>
> *about as sharp as a bowling ball*
>
> *full throttle, dry tank*
>
> *dumber than a box of hair*
>
> *dumb as a donkey*
>
> *as smart as bait*
>
> *missing a few buttons on his remote control*
>
> *dumber than paint*
>
> *half a bubble off plumb*

all crown and no filling

all wax and no wick

all foam, no beer

as much use as a lead parachute

not the brightest bulb on the Christmas tree

as useful as dinosaur repellent

as smart as a stick

as much use as an ashtray on a motorcycle

as quick as a corpse

all hammer, no nail

all belt, no trousers

focused like a 12-gauge shotgun

dumb as a stump

running on only 3 of his 4 cylinders

one putt short of par

one ski short of a snowmobile

about as sharp as a marble

always sharpening his sleeping skills

always at the right place at the wrong time

proof that evolution CAN go in reverse

His ...

elevator doesn't go all the way to the top floor

cursor's flashing, but there is no response

mouth is in gear, but his brain is in neutral

gates are down and the lights are flashing, but the train isn't coming

intellect is rivaled only by garden tools

driveway doesn't quite reach the road

antenna doesn't pick up all the channels

battery is not fully charged

receiver is off the hook

belt doesn't go through all the loops

engine is running, but nobody is behind the wheel

mind was shipped, but not delivered

She is a few ...

bricks short of a wall

gunmen short of a posse

flying buttresses short of a cathedral

screws short of a hardware store

sandwiches short of a picnic

threads short of a sweater

Bradys short of a bunch

clowns short of a circus

watts short of a light bulb

fruit loops shy of a full bowl

shades beyond blonde

toppings short of a Deluxe Pizza

burgers short of a barbecue

colors short of a rainbow

boats short of a fleet

noodles short of a chow mein

bristles short of a broom

boxes short of a pallet

pickles short of a jar

peas short of a casserole

cards short of a deck

fries short of a Happy Meal

beers short of a six-pack

keys short of a keyboard

fuses short of a full circuit

pecans short of a fruitcake

She ...

would lose a debate with a doorknob

has an IQ lower than plant life

would argue with a signpost

wouldn't know if she was on foot or horseback

doesn't have all the chairs at the table

couldn't figure her way through a maze, even with the mice helping her

needs her sleeves lengthened by a couple of feet so they can be tied in the back

does not have enough pages between the covers

couldn't hit the floor if she fell on it

hasn't seen the ball since kickoff

couldn't pour water out of a boot with instructions on the heel

has all the sex appeal of a wet paper bag

gets her orders from a different planet

fell out of the family tree

If ...

brains were bird droppings, he would have a clean cage

brains were dynamite, she wouldn't have enough to blow her nose

brains were water, his wouldn't be sufficient to baptize a flea

brains were taxed, she'd get a rebate

he was any more stupid, he would have to be watered twice a week

what you don't know can't hurt you, she's invulnerable

his IQ was two points higher, he'd be a rock

you gave them a penny for their thoughts, you'd get change

she had another brain it would be lonely

he was any smarter, he would be retarded

And ...

not all his soldiers are marching in line

during evolution her family was in the control group

the lights are on but no one is home

if you stand close enough to him, you can hear the sea

the logs are ablaze but the chimney is clogged

the wheel is spinning, but the hamster fell off

the wind is blowing, but nothing is moving

the umbrella is up, but there's no rain

most people drink from the fountain of knowledge, but she's only gargled

When they are together they are not the ...

brightest lights in the harbor

sharpest knives in the drawer

most colorful crayons in the box

fastest ships in the fleet

Chapter Five

The Helping Hand Strikes Again: Therapy and Other Unnatural Acts

There is no psychiatrist in the world like a puppy licking your face.
—Attributed to Ben Williams

Therapy is a strange phenomenon. For a short period of time—approximately an hour a week, client and therapist come together to discuss intimate subjects such as family history, relationships, sexuality, finances, emotions, and self-defeating behaviors. To the patient, it's as though the therapist is speaking in tongues. To the therapist, it's like steering a loaded luggage cart with one bad wheel through an airport. Sometimes therapy feels ridiculous, and sometimes it must look ridiculous.

The following humor embodies some valuable truths, and illustrates reasons why psychotherapy is not an exact science.

* * *

"Doctor, I'm terribly worried. I keep seeing pink striped crocodiles every time I try to sleep."

"Have you seen a psychiatrist?" asked the physician. "No, only pink striped crocodiles," replied the woman.

* * *

After running a series of tests, the psychiatrist said to the male patient, "You have something seriously wrong with your brain. You will need a brain transplant immediately. We have female and male brains. The female brains are $500.00 and the male brain is $5,000.00."

"What's the difference between a male and female brain?" the man asked. "The difference is that the female brain is used," replied the doctor.

* * *

A man who thinks he's George Washington had been seeing a counselor. The client finished up the session by saying, "Tomorrow we'll cross the Delaware and surprise them when they least expect it."

As soon as he was gone, the counselor picked up the phone and said, "King George. This is Benedict Arnold. I have the plans."

* * *

Blonde: I'm on the road a lot, and my clients are complaining that they can never reach me.

Psychiatrist: Don't you have a phone in your car?

Blonde: That was a little too expensive, so I did the next best thing. I put a mailbox in my car.

Psychiatrist: Um ... How's that working?

Blonde: Actually, I haven't gotten any letters yet.

Psychiatrist: And why do you think that is?

Blonde: I figure it's because when I'm driving around, my zip code keeps changing.

* * *

A New York psychiatrist ran into one of his patients at a restaurant.

"Doctor," the woman said while introducing her spouse, "this is my husband—one of the men I've been telling you about."

* * *

A woman sat down in a therapist's office. "I think I might be a nymphomaniac," she said.

"I see. Well, I can help you, but I ought to tell you in advance that my fee is $150 an hour."

"Hmmm," she said, "how much for all night?"

* * *

Group therapy is where 10 people get together to solve their own problems—and at $60 a person, the therapist's too!

* * *

Smoke poured through the apartment building, fire engines came clanging to the scene, and tenants ran to the street in their night clothes carrying whatever possessions they could grab. One of the tenants noticed that the man who lived in the apartment next to hers was carrying a covered bird cage and asked, "What do you have in the cage?"

"That's my pet rooster," he replied. "Rooster!" the woman gasped. Later she told a solicitous neighbor, "Can you beat that! I've been going to a therapist for months to cure me of the delusion that I keep hearing a rooster crow."

* * *

Therapists are likely to encounter just about anything. There was the man who walked into a mental health clinic stark naked and said, "I wish you could tell me why it is that whenever I walk through the streets people keep staring at me."

* * *

"Doctor, my trouble is that I dream the same dream over and over. I'm in a girls' dormitory, and the girls run from room to room stark naked."

"Very interesting," said the therapist. "No doubt you want me to help you get rid of these dreams about naked women?"

"Oh, no," said the client, "not that. I just want these girls to stop slamming doors and waking me up just when I'm about to catch one of them."

* * *

A talkative woman was telling her husband about her new therapist. "If that man yawned once while I was talking to him, he yawned 20 times."

"Maybe," said the husband, "he wasn't yawning. Maybe he was trying to say something."

* * *

After months of treating a client, the therapist said, "Now you are cured. You will no longer have delusions of grandeur and imagine that you're Napoleon."

The client replied, "That's wonderful. The first thing I'm going to do is to call Josephine and tell her the good news."

* * *

A therapist once asked his client if she ever suffered from fantasies of self-importance.

The client replied, "No, on the contrary. I think of myself as much less than I really am."

* * *

A fellow walked into a therapist's office looking depressed. "Doc, you have to help me. I can't go on like this."

"What's the problem?" the doctor inquired. "Well, I'm 35," the man replied, "and I have no luck with the ladies. I think I scare them away."

"This is serious," said the doctor. "You'll have to work on your self-esteem. Every morning look into the mirror and tell yourself you are a good person, a fun person, and an attractive person. Say it out loud with conviction. Within a week, you'll have women swarming all over you." The man seemed content with the advice and walked out of the office filled with excitement.

Three weeks later he returned with the same downtrodden look on his face. "Did you take my advice?" asked the doctor. "Well," said the man, "it worked all right. For the past three weeks, I enjoyed some of the best moments of my life with the most beautiful women."

"So what's the problem?" inquired the doctor.

"I don't have a problem," said the man. "My wife does."

* * *

A fellow was feeling down about himself and went to see a therapist. The therapist asked him a few questions, took some notes, and then sat in silence for a few minutes with a puzzled look on his face.

"I think your problem is low self-esteem. It's very common among losers."

* * *

Psychiatrist to nurse:

Just say we are running late. Don't keep saying it's a mad house around here.

* * *

I know a psychologist who just went bankrupt. People kept giving him a penny for his thoughts!

* * *

A patient was brought to a psychiatrist by friends who informed the doctor that the man was suffering from delusions of a huge fortune awaiting him. He was expecting two letters that would give him details involving the deeds to a rubber plantation in Sumatra and the titles to some mines in South America.

"It was a difficult case, and I worked hard on it," the psychiatrist told some colleagues. "And just when I had the man cured—the two letters arrived."

* * *

Neurotics build castles in the sky. Psychotics live in them. Psychiatrists collect the rent.

* * *

Psychologist to patient:

"We've made great strides in your case, Mr. Anderson. Originally, it was thought that phobias such as this were the result of a chemical imbalance in the brain. Now we've progressed to the point where we don't know what causes it."

* * *

A wealthy woman was in her therapist's office, terribly upset about a bad dream.

"Now," soothed the therapist, "Tell me about this dream you had."

"Well," said the lady, "I dreamed I was walking down the street with nothing on but a hat."

"And you were embarrassed?"

"Yes, I was," she said. "It was last year's hat!"

* * *

Counselor: You still think people are talking about you?

Client: For sure. Friday afternoon, I'm walking home from school and I'm watching some men build a new house.

Counselor: What's wrong with that?

Client: The guy hammering on the roof called me a paranoid little weirdo in Morse code.

* * *

The clinic secretary walks into the counselor's office. "Mr. Black is in the waiting room, and he claims he is invisible!"

"Tell him I can't see him," responds the counselor.

* * *

Counselor: Are you troubled by improper thoughts?

Client: Certainly not. I enjoy them!

* * *

A man fearful of a nervous breakdown was persuaded to consult a psychiatrist. After their first session, she gave him a list of things to do and made a weekly appointment for him. Two weeks later, the doctor telephoned him and asked why he had failed to keep his appointment.

"But, Doctor," he explained, "you said for me to stay away from people who irritate me, and I don't know anyone who irritates me more than you do."

* * *

Janet was so insecure that she often thought the car driving in front of her was following her, the long way around.

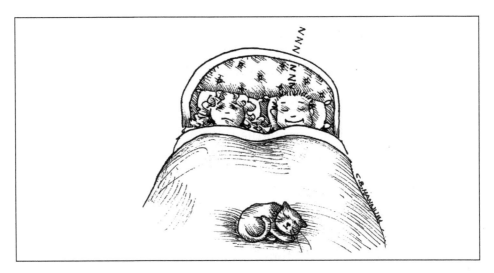

* * *

A young woman took her troubles to a psychiatrist. "Doctor, you must help me," she pleaded. "It's gotten so that every time I date a nice guy, I end up in bed with him. And then afterward, I feel guilty and depressed for a week."

"I see," nodded the psychiatrist. "And you, no doubt, want me to strengthen your will power and resolve in this matter."

"For God's sake, NO!" exclaimed the woman. "I want you to fix it so I won't feel guilty and depressed afterward."

* * *

Therapist: How's your insomnia?
Client: Worse. I can't even sleep when it's time to get up.

* * *

The social worker pointed out that most of the things his client was anxious about never actually came to pass. "I know," admitted the client sadly, "but then I worry about why they didn't happen."

* * *

A kindly psychiatrist assures every patient, "These pills don't have any side effects."

Unfortunately, it's just an M.D. promise.

* * *

"I've had a rough day. I put my shirt on, and a button fell off. I picked up my briefcase, and the handle fell off. I'm afraid to go to the bathroom."

* * *

Therapist: How do you feel about sex?

Woman: There's nothing wrong with sex. It's a perfectly natural, disgusting act.

* * *

"What's your problem?" asked the therapist.

"I think I'm a chicken," replied the patient.

"How long has this been going on?" the therapist inquired.

"Ever since I was an egg," said the client.

* * *

"I keep thinking I'm a dustbin," said the first patient.

"Don't talk such rubbish," replied the second patient.

* * *

A man was convinced he was dead, and it seemed that nothing could persuade him otherwise. When words failed, his psychotherapist resorted to text books; and after three hours of careful argument backed up by expert testimony, she got the man to agree that dead men don't bleed.

"So now," said the therapist, "I will prick your finger with a needle."

She jabbed a needle into the tip of the man's finger, and it started to bleed.

"What does that tell you?" asked the therapist triumphantly.

"That dead men *do* bleed," replied the man.

* * *

There was a patient whose name was Carol Kissinger. She hated the name, so she went to court and changed it to Smith. Two months later, she changed it to Johnson. Then after consultation with her counselor, she decided to change it to Loomis. By this time, all her friends had begun to ask, "I wonder who is Kissinger now?"

* * *

Patient: Doctor, Doctor, I think I'm a bridge.

Doctor: What's come over you?

Patient: Oh, two cars, a large truck and a bus.

* * *

Patient: Doctor, Doctor, I keep trying to get into fights.

Doctor: And how long have you had this complaint?

Patient: WHO WANTS TO KNOW?

* * *

Patient: Doctor, Doctor, I can't concentrate. One minute I'm OK, and the next minute, I'm blank!

Doctor: And how long have you had this complaint?

Patient: What complaint?

* * *

Patient: Doctor, Doctor, I keep thinking I am a set of curtains!

Doctor: Pull yourself together, man.

* * *

Patient: Doctor, Doctor, I keep thinking I'm a bell.

Doctor: Well, just go home; and if the feeling persists, give me a ring.

* * *

Patient: Doctor, Doctor, people tell me I'm a wheelbarrow.

Doctor: Don't let people push you around.

* * *

Patient: Doctor, Doctor, I've only got 59 seconds to live.

Doctor: Wait a minute, please.

* * *

Patient: Doctor, Doctor, I keep thinking I'm invisible.

Doctor: Who said that?

* * *

Patient: Doctor, Doctor, nobody understands me.
Doctor: What do you mean by that?

* * *

Patient: Doctor, Doctor, People keep ignoring me!
Doctor: Next!

* * *

Patient: Doctor, Doctor, no one believes a word I say.

Doctor: Tell me the truth now, what's your REAL problem?

* * *

Patient: Doctor, Doctor, I feel like a pack of cards.

Doctor: I'll deal with you later.

* * *

Patient: Doctor, Doctor, I keep thinking I'm a spoon.

Doctor: Sit there and don't stir.

* * *

Patient: Doctor, Doctor, I can't stop stealing things.

Doctor: Take these pills for a week; if that doesn't work, I'll have a color TV!

* * *

Patient: Doctor, Doctor, I think I'm schizophrenic.

Doctor: How long have you had this problem?

Patient: Please, I can't hear the doctor when you're all talking in my head!

* * *

Patient: Doctor, Doctor, I think I'm a toilet bowl.

Doctor: You are fine, just a little flushed.

* * *

Two women were comparing notes on their psychotherapist. "Frankly, mine drives me crazy," says Eileen. "Three years I've been going to her now and she never says a single word to me. She just sits there and nods."

"That's nothing," responded Ruthie, "After six years I finally get three words out of mine."

"Oh yeah? What'd he say?"

"No hablo Ingles."

—*Ronnie Shakes* (1992)

* * *

As the substance abuse counselor completed the intake evaluation of a patient, he said, "I can't find the cause of your complaint. Frankly, I think it's due to drinking."

"In that case," said the client, "I'll come back when you're sober."

* * *

How many rational-emotive therapists does it take to change a light bulb?

Why should the light bulb necessarily have to change? Why can't it be happy the way it is?

* * *

How many psychologists does it take to change a light bulb?

None. The light bulb will change itself when it's ready.

* * *

How many clinical social workers does it take to screw in a light bulb?

Two. One to screw it in, and one to tell him in he is screwing it in the wrong way.

* * *

How many marriage counselors does it take to change a light bulb?

Just one, but it takes nine visits.

* * *

How many psychiatric nurses does it take to change a light bulb?

One, but she must consult the DSM.

* * *

How many psychiatrists does it take to change a light bulb?

How long have you been having this fantasy?

* * *

How many psychoanalysts does it take to change a light bulb?

How many do *you* think it takes?

* * *

How many existentialist therapists does it take to change a light bulb?

Two: One to screw it in, and another to observe how the light bulb symbolizes a single incandescent beacon of subjective reality in netherworld of endless absurdity reaching out toward a maudlin cosmos of nothingness.

* * *

How many recovering addicts does it take to screw in a light bulb?

Two: One to screw it in, and one to sponsor him.

* * *

How many dyslexics does it take to bulb a light change?

Eno.

* * *

"I have good news and bad news for you," said the therapist to the client.

"Lay it on me. What's the bad news?" responded the client.

The therapist stated, "You have Alzheimer's Disease."

"That's terrible. What's the good news?" replied the client.

"You can go home and forget about it," said the therapist.

* * *

I'm in denial about the fact I'm in therapy. I just convince myself there's a friend I see once a week, and then I lend her $90.00 dollars, and she never pays me back.

—*Caroline Rhea* (2009)

* * *

A woman went to a therapist. "I wish you would see my husband. He's out of his mind. He blows smoke rings all the time."

"What's so unusual about that?" asked the therapist. "I do it myself."

"But," she said, "he doesn't smoke."

* * *

Nurse: The best time to take this anti-depression medication is just before retiring.

Patient: You mean I don't have to take it until I'm 65 years old?

* * *

Psychotherapist to voluptuous client leaving office: "That about winds things up. Any inhibitions you have left you're going to need."

* * *

There is this nervous client whose imagination afflicts him with all kinds of ills that never materialize. One afternoon he staggers into the local mental health clinic. Bent forward, he totters to a chair, and curls up into a half-moon shape. "Doctor," he gasps, "it has come at last. There was no warning. All of a sudden I found I couldn't straighten up. I can't lift my head."

Client: Last night I dreamt I was a teepee.
The night before, I dreamt that I was a wigwam.
Social Worker: Relax. Your're too tense.

As the doctor examines him he asks, "Is there any hope?"

"Well" the doctor said, "It will help a great deal if you will unhitch the third buttonhole of your vest from the top button of your pants."

* * *

A man came into a therapist's office with two badly burned ears. "I was ironing my shirt when the phone rang," he explained. "I accidentally reached for the iron instead of the phone and put it to my ear."

"I could understand if one of your ears was burned by the iron," said the counselor. "But two?"

"Well," the man sighed, "the phone rang again."

* * *

Summoning the patient into his office, the psychiatrist shot her a radiant smile.

"You know, Claudia, in this profession one rarely uses the word 'cure.' But after five years of therapy, it is my pleasure to pronounce you one hundred percent cured!" he proudly announced.

To his surprise, an unhappy look came over the woman's face.

"What's wrong?" asked the doctor. "This is a success for me and a triumph for you. I thought you'd be thrilled."

"Oh, its fine for you," she finally snapped, "but look at it from my point of view. Three years ago I was Joan of Arc. Now I'm nobody."

✳ ✳ ✳

Hello, and welcome to the mental health hotline.

If you are obsessive-compulsive, press 1 repeatedly.

If you are co-dependent, please ask someone to press 2 for you.

If you have multiple personalities, press 3, 4, 5 and 6.

If you are paranoid, we know who you are and what you want. Stay on the line, so we can trace your call.

If you are delusional, press 7, and your call will be transferred to the mother ship.

If you are schizophrenic, listen carefully and a small voice will tell you which number to press.

If you are manic-depressive, it doesn't matter which number you press. No one will answer.

If you have a nervous disorder, please fidget with the hash key until someone comes on the line.

If you are dyslexic, press 6969696969.

If you have amnesia, press 8 and state your name, address, phone number, date of birth, social security number, and your mother's maiden name.

If you have post-traumatic-stress disorder, slowly and carefully press 000.

If you have bipolar disorder, please leave a message after the beep or before the beep or after the beep. Please wait for the beep.

If you have short-term memory loss, press 9. If you have short-term memory loss, press 9. If you have short-term memory loss, press 9. If you have short-term memory loss, press 9.

If you have low self-esteem, please hang up. All our operators are too busy to talk to you.

If you are incontinent, please hold.

Have a nice day.

✳ ✳ ✳

A woman went to a counselor and confessed she was a kleptomaniac. He told her not to worry and gave her something to take.

* * *

A psychiatrist took his patient over to the window and asked her to stick out her tongue.

She did what he requested, then asked, "Why?"

"I don't like the psychiatrist across the street."

* * *

One week after moving into his own apartment, Tony, a shy introverted man, met with his community mental health worker. "I like the apartment but I'm not so sure I like the neighbors," said Tony.

Concerned that Tony have a positive experience, the worker asked about the neighbors.

"One woman cries all day, another lies in bed moaning. But the one who bothers me the most is the guy who keeps banging his head against the wall."

"You better keep away from them," warned the now very concerned worker.

"I am. I stay inside all day, playing my tuba."

* * *

The therapist said sternly to the patient. "If you think you're walking out of here cured after only three sessions, you're crazy."

* * *

William: I asked my psychiatrist, "How soon until I know I'm cured?"

Marta: What did she say?

William: She said, "The day you run out of money."

* * *

I have been coming to you for counseling for two years and all you do is listen to what I say. You never say anything back. I don't have to go to a psychotherapist for that. I could have stayed home with my husband. That's all he does too.

* * *

I wanted to go to Paranoids Anonymous meetings, but they wouldn't tell me where the group was meeting.

* * *

Razors pain you;

Rivers are damp;

Acids stain you;

And drugs cause cramp.

Guns aren't lawful; Nooses give;

Gas smells awful;

You might as well live.

—*Dorothy Parker* ("Résumé," 1925)

* * *

Cured patient to a psychologist: How can you tell me you don't want to see me anymore? I gave you the best years of my strife.

* * *

Did you hear about the self-help group for compulsive talkers? It's called On and On Anon.

* * *

I belong to a support group called Divorcees Anonymous. During those times I feel like leaving my wife, they send over an accountant to talk me out of it.

* * *

I joined Bridegrooms Anonymous. Whenever I feel like getting married, they send over a lady in a housecoat and hair curlers to burn my toast for me.

* * *

Joining Underachievers Anonymous wasn't very helpful. I think it's because it only has nine steps.

* * *

Overheard at Gamblers Anonymous Meeting:

"I'm going to the horse races, and I sure hope I break even."

"Break even, how come?" inquired a fellow member.

"I need the money."

* * *

"I'm so bad at putting things off, I finally joined Procrastinators Anonymous. Unfortunately, they haven't gotten around to having a meeting."

* * *

There are so many twelve-step groups today including AA (Alcoholics Anonymous) and ACA (Adult Children of Alcoholics). These are *not* inclusive enough. Here is a recovery program that covers all the bases.

ABCDEFGHIJKLMNOPQRSTUVWXYZ (Adult Bad Children of Dysfunctional Evil Families Getting Hooked Into Just Keeping Little Mean Nasty Old People Quiet Requiring Specialized Treatment Using Valium With eXtreme unYielding Zeal)

—*Guy Owen* (1996)

* * *

A clinic recently scheduled a seminar on Chronic Fatigue Syndrome. But it was a failure. Everybody was too tired to go.

* * *

Friend: You had a session with a shrink to cure your inferiority complex. Was it successful?

Patient: Well, yes and no. It cost me a hundred dollars for the session. Then it cost me a hundred and fifty dollars because I talked back to a traffic cop.

* * *

Any man who goes to a psychiatrist should have his head examined.

—*Attributed to Sam Goldwyn* (1969)

* * *

An airline pilot went to a sex therapist for a consultation. "When was the last time you had sex?" asked the therapist.

The pilot answered, "About 1955."

"That's a long time ago," responded the shocked therapist.

The pilot said, "That wasn't so long ago." He looked at his watch and went on, "It's only 2120!"

* * *

Therapy is wonderful. One of my friends was in therapy for five years and he turned his life around. He used to be depressed and miserable. Now he's miserable and depressed.

* * *

I told my wife the truth. I told her I was seeing a psychiatrist. Then she told *me* the truth. She was seeing a psychiatrist, two plumbers, and a bartender.

* * *

A fellow went to a therapist and told her he felt people were trying to take advantage of him.

"Don't worry about that," the therapist told him. "Everybody feels like people are trying to take advantage of them now and then. You're completely normal."

"Gee, thanks," the fellow said, "I feel better already."

"Terrific," responded the therapist. "That'll be one hundred dollars, and I need to borrow your car tonight."

* * *

Psychiatrist to patient: That will be $150.

Patient: Why $150? All the other psychiatrists in town charge $100.

Psychiatrist: It's part of the treatment. It will help you to attach less importance to money and marital things.

* * *

A bruised and battered client to his therapist:

"Yesterday I had a near-death experience that changed me forever."

"What happened?" asked the concerned therapist.

"It was a beautiful day and I went horseback riding. Everything was going fine until the horse started bouncing out of control. I tried with all my might to hang on but was thrown off."

He went on, "Just when things could not possibly get worse, my foot got caught in the stirrup. When this happened, I fell head first to the ground. My head continued to bounce harder as the horse didn't stop or even slow down. Just as I was giving up hope and losing consciousness, the Wal-Mart manager came and unplugged the damn thing."

***

I was walking across a bridge one day and I saw a man standing on the edge, about to jump off. So I ran over and said, "Stop! Don't do it."

"Why shouldn't I?" he asked.

"Well, there's so much to live for!" I said.

He said, "Like what?"

I said, "Well, are you religious or an atheist?"

He said, "Religious."

I said, "Me too! Are you Christian or Buddhist?"

He said, "Christian."

I said, "Me too! Are you Catholic or Protestant?"

He said, "Protestant."

I said, "Me too. Are you Episcopalian or Baptist?"

He said, "Baptist."

"Wow!" I said. "Me too! Are you Baptist Church of God or Baptist Church of the Lord?"

He said, "Baptist Church of God!"

"Me too!" I said. "Are you Original Baptist Church of God or are you Reformed Baptist Church of God?"

He said, "Reformed Baptist Church of God!"

I said, "Me too! Are you Reformed Baptist Church of God, Reformation of 1879, or Reformed Baptist Church of God, Reformation of 1915?"

He said, "Reformed Baptist Church of God, Reformation of 1915!"

I said, "Die, heretic scum," and pushed him off.

***

A very despondent young man living in Miami Beach went to a therapist for counseling.

"I can't seem to meet women," he complained, "I go to the beach every day and women ignore me. They are only interested in the guys with the big muscles."

Recently trained in solution-oriented therapy, the therapist felt confident he could be of help. "First, you need to do something that makes you stand out from the other guys," said the therapist. "Tomorrow put a banana in your bathing suit and walk up and down the beach."

The idea sounded a bit unorthodox but the young man was desperate and willing to do whatever the therapist suggested.

The following week he returned looking even glummer. "I did exactly what you told me to do," said the young man. "I put a banana in my Speedo and walked up and down the beach."

"That's exactly what I recommended. So what happened?" asked the therapist.

"It was awful," replied the discouraged fellow. "Guys laughed at me, and the women pointed and giggled."

Thinking for a minute, the therapist had an inspiration.

"Hmm, I think I figured out the problem. The next time you go the beach, put the banana in the front of your bathing suit."

✳ ✳ ✳

A man goes to a therapist. "My wife is unfaithful to me. Every evening she goes to Larry's bar and picks up men. In fact, she sleeps with anyone who asks her! I'm going crazy. What do you think I should do?"

"Relax," says the therapist, "take a deep breath and calm down. Now, tell me, where exactly is Larry's bar?"

Chapter Six

Kids and Ids:
Annoying Children

As soon as I stepped out of my mother's womb onto dry land, I realized that I had made a mistake—that I shouldn't have come. But the trouble with children is that they are not returnable.
　—Quentin Crisp (1968)

It has been said that three of the most difficult periods in a child's life are those years between 1 and 10, 10 and 20, and 20 and 30. After that, it just gets better.

Children and adolescents are a challenge to both parents and therapists. For the parents, the challenge becomes survival, and keeping one's perspective—sometimes under impossible conditions. For the therapists, the challenge is figuring out whether the behavior they are seeing is abnormal—or just the crazy stuff that normal kids go through.

As evident from the following humor, it's bad to be an orphan, miserable to be an only child, damaging to be the youngest, crushing to be the middle and terrible to be the oldest. There is no way out except to be born an adult.

* * *

The mother of a problem child was seen by a psychiatrist.

"You're far too upset about your son. I would like to put you on a tranquilizer."

On the next visit, the psychiatrist asked, "Has the tranquilizer calmed you down?"

"Yes," the boy's mother answered.

"And how's your son doing?" the psychiatrist asked.

"Who cares," said the mother.

* * *

Mrs. Rosenberg was so proud. "Did you hear about my son Leonard?" she asked Mrs. Bernstein. "He's going to a psychiatrist twice a week."

"Is that good?" queried Mrs. Bernstein.

"Good?" exclaimed Mrs. Rosenberg. "Of course it's good. Not only does he pay $100.00 an hour, but all he talks about is me!"

* * *

Special Education Teacher: Use the word 'fascinate' in a sentence.

Child: There are ten buttons on my coat, but I can only fasten eight.

* * *

"You know something, Mom," said the child, "I think my therapist is dumb."

"How can you say something like that?" asked the mother.

"Well, it's true," the child continued, "today I drew a picture of a rabbit with five ears and six eyes and when she looked at it, she said, "Now, what do you suppose this is?"

* * *

"What kind of a childhood did you have?" asked the counselor.

"Terrible! I was pretty stupid," replied the client.

"Give me an example," said the counselor.

"Well," replied the client, "for one, I didn't realize I was twelve until I was fourteen."

* * *

Two children were sitting on the front porch talking about families.

One asked the other, "Do you believe in planned parenthood?"

The other replied, "I sure do. I wish I could have planned mine."

* * *

The parents of a difficult boy were discussing what to give him for a birthday present. The mother said, "Let's buy him a bike."

"Well," said the father, "maybe—but do you think it will improve his behavior?"

"Probably not," said the mother. "But it will spread it over a wider area."

* * *

The parents of children who attend a local Montessori School gathered one night to hear a lecture by a child psychiatrist. After she finished, she called for questions and patiently handed out advice on behavior problems.

The pleasant evening broke up as a grim-faced father in the back seat arose and asked seriously, "Doctor, how do you feel about capital punishment?"

* * *

Some towns are really kid friendly. Take Cambridge MA—it's the kind of place where you can walk into a children's bookstore and find a Self-Help section. There is a book for five-year-olds called *Learning to Tie Your Inner Shoe*.

—*Jonathon Katz* (2009)

* * *

A kid says to his father, "I want to grow up and be a therapist."

The father replies, "You can't have it both ways."

* * *

"I found some contraceptives on the patio," said the first kid.

"What's a patio?" asked the second kid.

* * *

Older woman to child.

"How old are you?"

"Seven," replied the child.

"You should be ashamed of yourself," said the woman. "When I was your age, I was ten!"

* * *

"My brother was arrested at the zoo this afternoon," said the client.

"Arrested? How come?" asked the therapist.

"Feeding the pigeons," was the response.

"But, what's wrong with that?" inquired the therapist.

"He was feeding them to the lions," said the client.

* * *

A psychiatrist was conducting a group therapy session with four young mothers and their small children.

"You all have obsessions," he observed.

To the first mother, Mary, he said, "You are obsessed with eating. You've even named your daughter Candy."

He turned to the second mom, Ann, and said, "Your obsession is with money. Again, it manifests itself in your child's name, Penny."

He turns to the third mom, Joyce. "Your obsession is alcohol. This too, manifests itself in your child's name, Brandy."

At this point, the fourth mother, Kathy, gets up, takes her little boy by the hand and whispers, "Come on, Dick, we're leaving."

* * *

One night a teenage girl brought her new boyfriend home to meet her parents. They were appalled by his appearance: leather jacket, motorcycle boots, tattoos, and pierced nose. Later, the parents pulled their daughter aside and confessed their concerns.

"Dear," said the mother diplomatically, "he doesn't seem very nice."

"Mom," replied the daughter, "if he wasn't nice, why would he be doing 5000 hours of community service?"

* * *

The mother of the small boy talking to a child psychiatrist:

"Well, I don't know whether or not *he* feels insecure, but everybody else in the neighborhood certainly does!"

* * *

Two mothers discussing their children over lunch at a country club:

"My son has never been to a therapist," the first mom proudly announced.

"Why? What's wrong with him?" asked the second mom.

* * *

A teacher noticed that one little boy was drawing everything in heavy black crayon. He drew black horses, black cows, and black barns.

Disturbed about what was going on in his mind, she called a meeting of the little boy's parents, the school's principal, and a school social worker.

They finally got at the root of the trouble—it was the only crayon he had.

* * *

Child to psychiatrist:

"It's about my father, actually—he's got this fixation that a *cow* can orbit the moon!"

* * *

Once upon a time, a four-year-old boy was visiting his aunt and uncle. He was a very outspoken little boy, and often had to be guided to say the right thing at the right time.

One day at lunch, when the aunt had company, the little boy said, "Auntie, I want to tinkle." Auntie took the little boy aside and said, "Never say that, Sonny. If you want to tinkle, say, 'I want to whisper.'" And the incident was forgotten.

That night when Uncle and Auntie were soundly sleeping, the little boy climbed into bed with them. He tugged at his uncle's shoulder and said, "Uncle, I want to whisper." The uncle said, "All right, Sonny, don't wake Auntie up. Whisper in my ear."

The little boy was sent back to his parents the next day and to a child guidance clinic the following day.

* * *

"I wouldn't worry about your son playing with dolls," the therapist told the middle-aged matron.

She said, "I'm not worried, but his wife is very upset."

* * *

"I think it's about time we talked about the facts of life," said the father to his child.

"Certainly," said the child, "what do you want to know?"

* * *

Little Johnny came running into the house and asked, "Mommy, can little girls have babies?"

"No," said his mom, "of course not."

Little Johnny then ran back outside, and his mom heard him yell to his friends.

"It's okay; we can play that game again."

* * *

First woman: "What if I have a baby, and I dedicate my life to it and it grows up to hate me, and it blames everything wrong with its life on me?"

Second woman: "What do you mean IF?"

* * *

A lot of kids in the United States are suffering from depression. Younger and younger, our children are seeing the Sippy-cup as half empty.

—*Maria Bamford* (2009)

* * *

The boss of a big company needed to call one of his employees about an urgent problem. He dialed the employee's home phone number and was greeted with a child's whispered, "Hello?"

The boss asked, "Is your Daddy home?"

"Yes," whispered the small voice.

"May I talk with him?" the man asked. To his surprise, the small voice whispered, "No."

"Is your Mommy there?"

"Yes."

"May I talk with her?"

"No."

"Is there any one there besides you?" the boss asked the child.

"Yes," whispered the child. "A policeman."

Wondering what a cop would be doing at his employee's home, the boss asked, "May I speak with the policeman?"

"No, he's busy," whispered the child.

"Busy doing what?"

"Talking to Daddy and Mommy and the fireman," came the whispered answer.

Growing worried as he heard what sounded like a helicopter through the earpiece on the phone, the boss asked, "What is that noise?"

"A hello-copper," answered the whispering voice.

"What is going ON there?" asked the boss, now alarmed.

In an awed whisper, the child answered, "The search team just landed the hello-copper."

Now really alarmed, the boss asked, "Why are THEY there?"

Still whispering, the young voice replied along with muffled giggle, "They're looking for me!"

＊＊＊

If I ever told my father,"I'm trying to get my head on straight," he would have knocked it off for me.

＊＊＊

My father used to play games with me as a kid. He used to throw me in the air, and walk away.

＊＊＊

Father: If you kids don't stop making so much noise, I'll go deaf.

Child: Too late. We stopped an hour ago.

There was a set of eight-year-old twins. One was the most pessimistic child in the town, while the other was the most optimistic.

Frustrated, the parents consulted a child therapist, and it was suggested they try an experiment. At Christmas, the parents gave the pessimistic twin everything he asked for. There was a bike, games, toys, and a train set, all for him. For the optimistic twin, the parents filled a box with horse manure, gift wrapped it, and put it under the large tree.

When the young pessimist opened his presents, he began to weep. "What's wrong?" asked the mother. "Oh, the presents are nice," the child replied, "but they'll just get broken."

When the young optimist opened his present, he whooped and hollered with joy and began to fling the manure in the air. The mother was shocked. "Why are you so excited about a box of horse manure?"

"Don't you see, Mom?" he answered. "With all this horse manure, there has to be a pony in the house somewhere."

＊＊＊

A woman was entertaining three other ladies at tea when her nine-year-old son burst into the room decked out in a shimmering white evening dress, a flowered hat, rouge on both cheeks, and his mouth smeared with lipstick.

"Wilfred, you nasty boy," cried the horrified mother."Go upstairs and take off your father's clothes this very instant."

＊＊＊

Self-absorbed teenager girl goes to confession:

"I'm so sinful, Father," she says. "Every time I look in the mirror, I think 'I'm so beautiful, I'm so beautiful, I'm so beautiful ...'"

"Go in peace, my child," says the priest. "It's not a sin. It's a delusion."

＊＊＊

"What's the trouble?" asked the gentleman of a little boy who was crying bitterly.

"My mom lost her psychology books," he explained between sobs, "and now she is using her good judgment."

＊＊＊

The mother was having a hard time getting her son to go to school in the morning.

"Nobody in school likes me," he complained. "The teachers don't like me, the kids don't like me, the superintendent wants to transfer me, the bus drivers hate me, the school board wants me to drop out, and the custodians have it in for me. I don't want to go to school."

"But you have to go to school," countered his mother. "You are healthy, you have a lot to learn, you have something to offer the others, you're a leader. And besides, you are 45-years-old and you are the principal."

＊＊＊

Before I got married I had six theories about bringing up children; now I have six children and no theories.

—*Attributed to John Wilmot, Earl of Rochester, 1647-1680*
(Wilmot 1989)

* * *

Howard, a retired psychologist, was doing a little neighborly kindness. The mother who lived next door had invited him over to talk to her little girl who she thought had a few abnormal tendencies. Being a jovial person he asked the child if she was a girl or a boy.

"A boy," she replied.

So, he tried again by asking her when she grew up what would she be a man or a woman.

The girl replied, "A man."

The mother saw he wasn't getting any place so she excused him. Then she asked her daughter, "Why did you give such strange answers?"

"Well," the little girl answered, "If he was going to ask stupid questions I was going to give him some stupid answers."

* * *

A most indulgent mother visiting a department store took her son to the toy department. Spying a gigantic rocking horse, he climbed up on it and rocked back and forth for almost an hour. "Come on, son," the mother pleaded. "I have to get home to get your father's dinner."

The little boy refused to budge, and her efforts were to no avail. The store clerks and the department manager, using all the psychology they knew, coaxed the little boy, without success. Eventually, out of desperation, they called the store's consulting psychologist who hap-

A research psychologist had twins. She rang the minister who was delighted.

"Bring them to church on Sunday, and we'll baptize them," said the minister.

"No," said the psychologist. "We'll baptize one and keep the other as a control."

pened to be in the building. He gently walked over to the lad and whispered a few words in his ear. The boy immediately jumped off and ran to his mother's side.

"How did you do it?" the mother asked incredulously. "What did you say to him?"

The psychologist hesitated for a moment then said. "All I said was, 'If you don't get off that rocking horse at once son, I'll knock the stuffing out of you!'"

* * *

They didn't believe in heredity until they produced this brilliant, good-looking child.

* * *

During a dinner party the host's two little children entered the dining room totally nude and slowly walked around the table. The parents, most embarrassed, pretended that nothing was happening and kept the conversation going. The guests cooperated and continued talking, totally ignoring the children.

After walking twice around the room, the children left and there was a moment of silence at the table, during which one child was heard to say, "You see, it *is* vanishing cream."

* * *

A social worker leading a group of six pre-delinquent boys was trying to teach them the evils of alcohol. To make his point, he put a worm in a glass of water and a second worm in a glass of whiskey. The worm in the water lived, and the worm in the whiskey died.

"All right, boys," asked the worker, "What does this show you?"

"Well," said one of the more outspoken members, "it shows me that if you drink whiskey, you won't have worms."

* * *

There was a child who never spoke. His parents hired famous doctors and therapists to examine him, but none could find a reason for his silence. One day when he was eight-years-old he put down the glass of milk he'd been drinking and said quite clearly: "This milk is sour."

The parents were shocked. "But you can speak!" said the astounded father. "Why haven't you ever spoken before?"

"Up until now," he said, "everything has been okay."

* * *

A precocious nine-year-old girl was sitting at the dining room table writing an essay on "Where My Family Came From" for her class.

"Mom, where did I come from?" she asked.

Her mother, a bit old-fashioned, answered, "Well, the stork brought you, dear."

"Then, where did *you* come from?"

"Uh, the stork brought me too."

"Okay, then where did Granny come from?"

"The stork brought her too."

"Okay," answered the girl, who settled down to complete her homework.

About five minutes later the mother happened to walk by her daughter and read the first sentence of the essay: "For three generations there have been no natural births in our family."

* * *

I've developed a new philosophy ... I only dread one day at a time.

—*Charles Schulz* (from *Peanuts: Charlie Brown,* 1985)

* * *

The teacher explained the meaning of the word *responsibility* to her second grade class. To reinforce the lesson, she then asked the children to tell about their responsibilities at home. The first hand to go up was that of a most mischievous little boy. "My responsibility," he proudly announced, "is to get out and stay out."

* * *

A second grader came home from school and said to her mother, "Guess what Mom? We learned to make babies today."

The very surprised mother tried not to overreact. "That's most interesting, darling," she said, "How do you make babies?"

"It's simple," replied the girl. "You just change *y* to *i* and add *es*."

* * *

Conversation overheard in the waiting room of a child guidance clinic:

Mother: Relax, Janie. Calm down, Janie. Take it easy, Janie.

Therapist walking by: I'm impressed the way you keep your temper while your little Janie is acting up.

Mother: Her name is Jennifer. I'm Janie.

* * *

At a parent-teacher conference, an overly protective mother told the teacher, "My son Paul is a very sensitive boy."

"Yes," said the teacher, "I've noticed that. Is there anything we should do about it?"

"Well," said the mother, "If Paul misbehaves, please spank the boy next to him."

* * *

A woman takes her eight-year-old son to a psychologist who specializes in learning problems of children. "He's got attention deficit disorder, doctor."

"Right," says the psychologist," and what do you think is the cause?"

"I'm going bowling tonight," replies the mother.

✳ ✳ ✳

Insanity is hereditary; you can get it from your children.

—*Sam Levenson* (1979)

✳ ✳ ✳

Concerned father talking to a psychiatrist:

"Doctor, I would like you to evaluate my 13-year-old son."

"OK," replied the doctor. "He's suffering from a transient psychosis with an intermittent rage disorder, punctuated by episodic radical mood swings, but his prognosis is good for full recovery."

"That's incredible," said the shocked father, "How can you say all that without ever meeting him?"

"I thought you said he is a 13-year-old."

✳ ✳ ✳

Two youngsters, both aged six, decide to get married. The boy goes to his father and tells of his plans. "How will you support her?" asks the father.

"Well," said the lad, "I get fifty cents a week allowance and she also gets an allowance."

"Where will you live?"

"We thought about that, I can live here with you and mom and she can live with her mom and dad."

"Interesting," replies the father, starting to get nervous. "But, what if there is a baby?"

"Bite your tongue, Dad. So far we've been lucky."

✳ ✳ ✳

Phillip, a six-year-old boy, comes home from school with a note from the teacher that says, "Phillip does not have an inquiring mind."

The mother is furious. "You're going to have an inquiring mind. I'm going to make you have an inquiring mind. If I have to beat you, you'll have an inquiring mind."

"What's an inquiring mind?" the little youngster asks.

"Shut up and don't ask so many questions!"

* * *

When I was a kid I used to love to sit at home in front of a roaring fire. Boy did that make my father mad. We didn't have a fire place.

* * *

They are now selling a teenage doll. You wind it up and it resents you for it.

* * *

Counselor: What's the biggest problem for young people today, lack of knowledge or apathy?

Adolescent Client: I don't know and I don't care.

* * *

There was a 16-year-old who was having run-ins with the law and always for the same offense: stealing motor scooters. So, the judge referred him to a therapist for an evaluation.

"What's his diagnosis?" asked the judge.

"Very simple," answered the therapist, "he's a chronic cycle-path."

* * *

There was a couple who enrolled their son in a boys activity group to help him learn to make decisions of his own. He did—the second session in the group he decided not to return.

Chapter Seven

All Family Problems Are Relative: Bewildering Relations

When I can no longer bear to think of victims of broken homes, I begin to think of the victims of intact ones.
    —Peter De Vries (1987)

The first half of our lives is dominated by our parents and the second half is dominated by our children. There are some who, if they had their druthers, would choose to have been born into a different family. Others swear they must have been switched at birth, or kidnapped as an infant and left on the porch of two peculiar people who insist on being called mom and dad. It's most disconcerting, once these same folks become parents and hear themselves repeat the threats, warnings, and ultimatums to their children that their parents used on them. This is often followed by, "Oh my God, I have become my mother."

Therapists have learned that most families are a lot like fudge—mostly sweet with a generous sprinkling of nuts scattered here and there. The following family humor puts some of the "fun" back into dysfunctional.

"Tell me about your disagreement," said the marriage counselor.

"In our six years of marriage," replied the husband, "we haven't been able to agree on anything."

"Wrong," said the wife, "it's been seven years, dear."

* * *

Her husband's odd habit was becoming unbearable. He just couldn't say a sentence without snapping his fingers. So the wife finally prevailed upon him to go to see a psychiatrist.

While the psychiatrist interviewed him, the exasperating quirk asserted itself.

"Are you happily married? Ever quarrel with your wife?"

"Oh, (snap) never. She's the finest woman a (snap) man could wish for."

"Get along with your boss?"

"Marvelously (snap). He's probably (snap) the most congenial (snap) boss in the City of New (snap) York."

"How about your father or mother?"

"No (snap) question about it; they were (snap) ideal parents."

Desperate, the doctor asked, "Then why this compulsion to snap your fingers?"

"Oh, (snap)," the patient replied, "I do that to keep the (snap) elephants away."

"But there isn't an elephant loose within 2000 miles of here!"

"You (snap) see?" said the patient, beaming. "Damned (snap) effective, what?"

∗ ∗ ∗

"Has there been any insanity in your family?" asked the therapist.

"Yes, doctor, my husband thinks he's the boss," replied the client.

＊＊＊

And then, of course, there is the one about the family who was very concerned because their daughter thought she was a chicken and ran around the house clucking. They were going to take her to a therapist, but they were poor and needed the eggs.

＊＊＊

A marriage counselor asked his new client why he hit his wife.

The man replied, "Her back was turned, the broom was handy, and the back door was open."

＊＊＊

A therapist was interviewing a woman regarding her pending divorce.

"What are the grounds for your divorce?" he asked.

She replied, "About four acres and a nice little home in the middle of the property with a stream running by."

"No," he said, "I mean what is the foundation of this case?"

"It is made of concrete, brick and mortar," she responded.

"I mean," he continued, "what are your relations like?"

"I have an aunt and uncle living here in town, and so do my husband's parents."

He said, "Do you have a real grudge?"

"No," she replied, "we have a two-car carport and have never really needed one."

"Please," he tried again, "is there any infidelity in your marriage?"

"Yes, both my son and daughter have stereo sets. We don't necessarily like the music, but the answer to your questions is yes."

"Ma'am, does your husband ever beat you up?"

"Yes," she responded, "about twice a week. He gets up earlier than I do."

Finally, in frustration, the therapist asked, "Lady, why DO you want a divorce?"

"Oh, I don't want a divorce," she replied. "I've never wanted a divorce. My husband does. He says he can't communicate with me."

* * *

A husband and wife were at a party chatting with some friends when the subject of marriage counseling came up.

"Oh, we'll never need that. My wife and I have a great relationship," the husband explained. "She was a communications major in college, and I majored in theatre arts." He continued, "She communicates well, and I act like I'm listening."

* * *

The other night I said to my wife Ruth, "Do you feel the sex and excitement have gone out of our marriage?" Ruth said, "I'll discuss this with you after the next commercial."

—*Milton Berle* (1989)

* * *

"Surely," insisted the marriage counselor, "You must have said something to start the awful fight."

"No, not really." the husband replied. "My wife had tried a new recipe for dinner. And when she asked how I liked it, all I said was, 'It's okay, but it will never take the place of food.'"

* * *

A mild-mannered man was tired of being bossed around by his tyrannical wife, so he went to a counselor. The counselor said he needed to build his self-esteem; and so he gave him a book on assertiveness, which he read on the way home. He had finished the book by the time he reached his house.

The man stormed into the house and walked up to his wife.

Pointing a finger in her face, he said, "From now on, I want you to know that I am the man of this house, and my word is law! I want you to prepare me a gourmet meal tonight, and when I'm finished eating my meal, I expect a sumptuous dessert afterward."

"Then," the man continued, "after dinner, you're going to draw my bath so I can relax. And, when I'm finished with my bath, guess who's going to dress me and comb my hair?"

The wife answered, "The funeral director."

* * *

When Joe's wife ran away with his car, his money, and his best friend, he got so depressed that his doctor sent him to a psychiatrist. Joe told the psychiatrist his troubles and said, "Life isn't worth living. I think I'm gonna kill myself."

"Don't be stupid, Joe," said the psychiatrist. "My wife ran off and left me, too, yet I'm happy."

"How?" asked Joe.

"Easy," replied the therapist. "I threw myself into my work. I totally submerged myself in my job and soon forgot her. By the way, Joe, what work do you do?"

"I clean out septic tanks," Joe replied.

* * *

A wife went in to see a therapist:

"I've got a big problem," she said. "Every time we're in bed and my husband climaxes, he lets out this earsplitting yell."

"My dear, that's completely natural," said the therapist. "I don't see what the problem is."

"The problem is," she complained, "it wakes me up."

* * *

"Good morning doctor," the man said. "I'm here because my wife insists that I need professional help."

"Why does she feel that way?" asked the doctor.

"Because I prefer bow ties to long ties," the man answered.

"I don't understand," the doctor said. "Why would she see that as a problem? Many people prefer bow ties to long ties. In fact, I have the same preference myself."

"Really?" the patient said, smiling. "How do you like yours—boiled or sautéed with a little garlic?"

* * *

The husband and wife go to a counselor after 15 years of marriage. The counselor asks them what the problem is.

The wife goes into a tirade, listing every problem they have ever had in the 15 years they've been married. She goes on and on and on.

Finally, the counselor gets up, goes around the desk, embraces the woman and kisses her passionately. The woman shuts up and sits quietly in a daze.

The counselor turns to the husband and says, "That is what your wife needs at least three times a week. Can you do that?"

The husband thinks for a moment and replies, "Well, I can get her here to your office Monday and Wednesday, but Friday I golf."

* * *

A wife went to a therapist in an attempt to sort out her sex life. For over half an hour, she talked about how unrewarding sex was with her husband; but the therapist was struggling to reach the root of the problem.

"Do you ever watch your husband's face while you're making love?" he asked.

"I did once," she replied.

"And how did he look?"

"Very angry."

"That's interesting. You say you have only once seen your husband's face during sex? That in itself is unusual. Tell me, what were the circumstances that led you to see his face on the occasion he appeared so angry?"

"He was looking through the window at me."

* * *

An old couple who'd been married more than 60 years got divorced in their 90's.

When asked why they had left it so late, the wife replied, "We wanted to wait until the children were dead."

* * *

She got a divorce on the grounds that her husband had only spoken to her three times in the course of seven years of marriage. She also got custody of the three children.

* * *

"What is the problem in the marriage?" asked the marriage counselor.

"I'm afraid my wife and I are incompatible," the husband replied.

"What do you mean by incompatible?" the counselor inquired.

"I want a divorce, and she doesn't," said the husband.

* * *

After 35 years of marriage, a husband announced that he wanted a divorce. His wife was stunned.

"But, John," she pleaded, "why would you divorce me after all we have been through together. Remember how after we met, you caught malaria and nearly died, but I looked after you? Then, when your family was wiped out in a hurricane, I was there for you."

She continued, "Then when you were falsely accused of armed robbery, I stood by you. And when you lost $40,000 on the horses, I sympathized. And when the fire destroyed your office, I comforted you. How could you leave me? We've been through so much?"

"That's the problem, Sue," replied the husband. "Face it, you're bad luck."

* * *

"The only thing my husband and I have in common is that we were married on the same day," said the woman to the marriage counselor.

* * *

"Is your husband hard to please?" asked the counselor.

"I don't know," replied the woman. "I've never tried."

* * *

"Tell me, Mr. Jackson," said the marriage counselor after several sessions, "did you wake up grouchy this morning?"

"No," said Mr. Jackson. "I let her sleep."

* * *

"My wife thinks she's a refrigerator!" said the frustrated husband.

"Don't worry, it will pass," said the social worker.

"But when she sleeps with her mouth open, that damn light bugs me!" replied the husband.

* * *

"Last week, you and your husband were considering a divorce," said the marriage counselor.

"Yes, but we changed our minds," responded the wife. "When we looked at the cost of the lawyers, we decided to put in a new swimming pool instead."

* * *

"I just about had enough of my wife saying she does everything for me," said the frustrated husband. He continued, "In fact, I'd leave tomorrow if I knew how to pack my suitcase."

* * *

"What kinds of things do you and your wife fight about?" asked the psychotherapist.

"I don't know," said the client. "She won't tell me."

* * *

"Last week I had an awful week," said the client to the social worker. "I am terribly suspicious that my wife is slowly becoming a nymphomaniac."

The social worker replied, "And you want me to stop it!"

"No," replied the client. "I want you to speed it up!"

* * *

A young woman phoned a friend and wept, "I just heard my husband wants a divorce."

"So what?" asked her sympathetic pal?

"Well," said the woman, "my therapist is out of town, and I just don't know what to *think!*"

* * *

The patient was trying to explain his unhappiness to a therapist.

"I have a son at Harvard and a daughter at Yale. I bought them both sports cars, and my wife a new Buick, and myself a new Italian racing car. I have a town house, a summer house in the country, and a cottage at the shore ... "

"But that all sounds pretty good to me," interrupted the therapist.

"I suppose so," said the man, "but I only make $300 a week."

* * *

A man came into his therapist's office with his head heavily bandaged.

"What happened to you?" asked the therapist.

"I was playing golf yesterday with my mother-in-law," he replied, "and on the second hole, she sliced her ball into a field full of cows."

He continued, "Because it was her favorite golf ball and she didn't want to lose it, she insisted that we search. We looked for a quarter of an hour, but there was no sign of it, just one old cow."

"Still," he went on, "my mother-in-law insisted that she wouldn't leave until we found her ball, so we kept on searching, but couldn't find it."

The client continued the saga.

"I was ready to give up when I thought to check that the ball hadn't somehow got lodged in the cow. So, I lifted up the cow's tail, and sure enough, a ball was stuck there. I called my mother-in-law over and said, 'Does this look like yours?' and she hit me in the head with a five iron."

* * *

"I got married because I was tired of going to the launderette, eating takeout food all the time, and always having holes in my socks," said the client.

The counselor responded, "That makes sense. But why did you get divorced?"

"For the same reasons," replied the client.

* * *

"How do you and your wife deal with conflict?" asked the counselor.

"That's simple," replied the client, "we never go to sleep angry with each other. We've been awake now for nearly six months."

* * *

In a group therapy session, a member related, "My grandfather predicted in advance the very year that he was going to die." He continued, "In fact, he predicted the very month, day, and hour."

"That's uncanny," responded the fellow next to him. "How did he know all that?"

"The judge told him," replied the member.

* * *

"You say your wife is very sentimental," said the therapist.

"Yes," responded the husband, "she got divorced in the same dress her mother got divorced in."

* * *

"My wife has been missing now for over a week, and I do so want her back," said the client to the marriage counselor.

"You're in pain because your heart is so full of love," empathized the counselor.

"Hell, no," responded the client, "because the sink is so full of dishes."

* * *

A couple had been married for 25 years.

One evening, the husband says, "Honey, let's go on a second honeymoon."

As he says this, he looks into the next room where an old lady sits knitting, and he says, "And this time, let's not take your mother."

His wife responds, "My mother. I thought she was your mother!"

* * *

A husband was having great difficulty getting along with his wife—nothing but arguing and friction—so he decided to consult a marriage counselor. After they had talked for a while, the counselor said, "I suggest that you run five miles each day of the week. Then please call me back."

A week later, the counselor received a call from the husband. "Well," asked the counselor, "how are things going with you and your wife?"

"How should I know?" said the husband. "I'm 35 miles away."

* * *

"I haven't spoken to my wife for 18 months," said the husband. "I don't like to interrupt."

* * *

A woman was applying for the renewal of her driver's license.

The inspector asked her, "Have you been adjudged insane or feeble-minded?"

He paused and smiled, then added, "That is, by anyone other than your own children?"

* * *

The wife of a farmer whose place was isolated in the vastness of the Kansas prairie suddenly went out of control and was placed in a state hospital. A social worker from the hospital visited the farm the next day to do a psycho-social history on the woman.

"What do you suppose pushed her over the edge?" asked the social worker.

"Beats the heck out of me," replied the farmer. "She hasn't been out of the kitchen in 20 years."

* * *

Middle-aged client during a group therapy session:

"Last night, my wife and I were sitting in the living room, and I said to her, 'I never want to live in a vegetative state, dependent on some machine and fluids from a bottle. If that ever happens, just pull the plug.'"

"She got up, unplugged the TV and then threw out my beer. She's such a Bitch ... "

* * *

"Doctor, my husband has a serious mental affliction. I notice when I have talked to him for an hour or so, he hasn't heard a word I said."

"Madam," soothed the therapist, "that's not an affliction. It's a gift."

* * *

Client: My ex-wife was fanatically tidy. She divorced me because I had one little hair out of place.

Therapist: That's not much of a reason to file for divorce.

Client: It was blond, and it was on my jacket.

* * *

"My wife had the strangest dream last night," said the fellow. He continued, "She dreamed she was married to a millionaire."

"You're lucky," his friend replied. "My wife dreams that in the daytime."

* * *

A doctor wanted to wean a woman off antidepressants. "What would happen if you stopped taking them?" he asked.

"To me, nothing," she said. "But all of a sudden my husband becomes a real jerk."

* * *

TOP 15 SIGNS YOU'VE HIRED THE WRONG MARRIAGE COUNSELOR

Degree on the wall reads, "Doctor of Swingology."

Keeps repeating, "If you can't change course, you must divorce."

"I'm afraid there's not much you can do with a penis that small."

Her latest book, Women Are From Venus, Men Are Lyin' Bastards.

"Just shut up and screw" doesn't seem like good advice.

After you've earned enough "session points," you get to choose either a Louisville Slugger or a Tazer Gun.

When you and your spouse claim sexual incompatibility, he throws a couple of pillows on the floor and says, "Prove it."

"Communication, schmunication—let's talk about 'backdoor love.'"

"Mr. and Mrs. Smith, Dr. Ike Turner will see you now."

You quickly discover that his motto, "Don't worry, be happy" is pretty much the extent of his knowledge of the English language.

Always takes Hillary Clinton's side.

In order to open the lines of communication, she begins the first session by hooking your genitals up to a car battery and tossing your wife the keys.

Agrees with husband that a request to "honk on Bobo" is foreplay enough.

Her last name has six hyphens.

—Chris White (2007)

* * *

Therapist to client:

"Mrs. Jones, I believe your husband is correct. You are a whiny bitch."

* * *

A woman walked into a New York bookstore. Unclear of a title, she asked the sales person for a book that was turned into a musical and which was still running on Broadway. "Do you have *Les Miserables*?"

"I'm not sure," said the sales person, "but look in the self-help and the psychology sections."

* * *

During a marriage counseling session the wife snapped at her husband: "That's not true! I do so enjoy sex." Then turning to the counselor she explained: "But this animal expects it once or twice a year!"

* * *

I'm thinking about going to an assertiveness training class. First, I need to check with my wife.

* * *

My wife has a terrible memory. She never forgets a thing.

* * *

I've got a superb memory. I can recite 10 pages of the New York City phone book by heart! Ready?

Smith, Smith, Smith, Smith …

* * *

There are two periods in a man's life when he doesn't understand women—before marriage and after marriage.

* * *

A man came into the office one morning looking very depressed. His associates asked him what the trouble was. "I'm suffering from a sexually transmitted disease."

There was an embarrassed silence until someone dared ask what it was.

"It's called life," he answered.

* * *

A wife called a psychotherapist and said, "My husband thinks he's Moses." The therapist assured her that delusions of grandeur were only a passing fancy.

"I hope so," says the wife, "but meanwhile, how can I keep him from parting the water when I take a bath?"

* * *

A woman explained to a therapist that her husband thought he was the Lone Ranger.

"How long has this been going on?" asked the therapist.

"About twenty years."

"It sounds very complicated," said the therapist, "but I believe I can cure him."

The woman nodded and said, "I guess it's the right thing to do. But Tonto is so good with the children."

* * *

A woman met with her counselor and complained, "This morning I went to the bathroom, and five pennies came out. This afternoon I went again and dimes and quarters fell out. I couldn't wait to get here."

"Take it easy," said the therapist. "You're just going through your change."

* * *

When two egotists marry you have the family dynamic of an *I for an I.*

* * *

"So," asked the marriage counselor, "why did you divorce your first wife?"

"As soon as we were married," said the man, "she cured me of drinking, smoking, and staying out till all hours. She also introduced me to the finer things like art and music. She taught me to dress well and master the rules of etiquette."

He went on, "Then, one morning I took a look at her and decided that she just wasn't good enough for me."

* * *

A man took his wife to a marriage counselor and said, "What's-her-name here complains that I don't give her enough attention!"

* * *

Two men meet on a bench in the park. The conversation gets around to women and marriage. One man says, "My wife is an angel. She doesn't drink or smoke, and spends half her time in church and comes home and sings hymns all evening long."

The second man says, "My wife was like that too. I strangled her."

* * *

Client to marriage counselor: I think my marriage is in big trouble.

Counselor: Why is that?

Client: I said to my wife, "Let's have some fun tonight, dear."

"Okay," she replied. "But please leave the light on in that hallway if you get home before I do."

* * *

A South American diplomat who was stationed in the United States had developed an impressively rich English vocabulary. However, feeling the stress of being thousands of miles from home and no one to confide, he went to see a psychotherapist specializing in family problems.

"Well," asked the therapist, "what bring you here today?"

"I'm having trouble with my wife," said the diplomat. "I love her very much."

"Ah," said the therapist, "tell me more."

"Well, we want to have some children, and, er, my wife seems to be—how you say?—*unbearable*."

"Unbearable?" asked the confused therapist.

"I mean *unscrutiable*," said the anxious gentleman.

"No, no," said the diplomat, "I mean *inconceivable*."

Seeing the blank look on the therapist face, he said, "What I mean, you see, is that she is—uh—oh, yes, *impregnable*."

* * *

A social worker recently reported that half her clients went to her because they weren't married and the other half went to her because they were.

* * *

Mrs. Virginia Walton called her insurance company to see if her policy covered psychiatric treatment. After reviewing her policy, the agent told her, "Yes, Virginia, there is an insanity clause."

* * *

Shortly after completing his training in marital counseling, a counselor was asked to speak to a young Couples Club on marital sex. The night of the speech, he returned home exhausted and immediately went upstairs to bed. As he brushed his teeth, his wife asked about the topic of his speech, and he mumbled the first thing that came into his mind—water skiing. Later in the week the wife was shopping at a local grocery store, and a friend came up to her and said how much the Couples Club enjoyed the speech.

"Frankly, I'm somewhat surprised," said the wife. "He's only tried it a few times. Once he got sick and the next time he fell off and broke his arm."

* * *

Women's letter to ex-husband

Dear Charlie,

> *I'm writing to say that I realize our divorce was entirely my fault. I still love you. I want you to know that if I ever get the chance, I would make it all up to you by being the most perfect wife you could ever hope to have. I finally realize how wonderful you are and how stupid I was to lose you.*

(Signed) Beverly

P.S. Congratulations on winning the lottery.

* * *

"I'm worried," said the mother to her therapist. "I caught my daughter and the boy next door examining each other's naked bodies."

"Oh, that's not unusual," smiled the therapist, "don't worry about it."

"But I am worried," insisted the woman, "and so is my daughter's husband."

* * *

"I had a terrible dream last night," said the client. "I dreamed I died and went to see St. Peter, and he told me if I'd never cheated on my wife I could drive a luxury car around heaven for ever. But, if I cheated twice I had to drive a compact car, and if I'd cheated three times I had to drive a sub-compact and if I'd cheated..."

"Hold on!" interrupted the therapist. "You've never cheated on your wife at all, have you?"

"Nope, and that's what I told Saint Peter. So he gave me this big luxury car with all the extras and off I drove."

"What's so bad about that?" asks the therapist. "It sounds like a great dream to me."

"Well, I was driving along in that thing and came on my wife. She was riding a bicycle with two flat tires."

* * *

An efficiency expert concluded his lecture on time-saving methods with a note of caution. "I suggest you do not try these techniques at home."

"Why not?" asked somebody from the audience.

"I watched my wife's routine at breakfast for years," the expert explained. "She made lots of trips between the refrigerator, stove, table and cabinets, often carrying a single item at a time. One day I told her, 'Hon, why don't you try carrying several things at once?'"

"Did it save time?" the person in the audience asked.

"Actually yes," replied the expert. "It used to take her 20 minutes to make the breakfast. Now I do it in seven."

* * *

Overheard during a women's support group:

I hate my aunts. During weddings, they'd poke me in the ribs and cackle, "You're next." They stopped after I started doing the same thing to them at funerals.

* * *

Also overheard during a women's support group:

"To tell the truth," said a stressed and overworked housewife, "I always wanted to have a nervous breakdown. But every time I was about to get around to it, it was time to fix somebody a meal."

* * *

Did you hear about the woman who confused her valium with her birth control pills? Now she has 14 kids but doesn't care.

* * *

A man with a very pronounced black eye goes to a marriage counselor. "What happened to your eye?" asked the counselor.

"Well," said the client, "that's why I'm here. Last night my wife and I were lying in bed and she says to me, 'If I died, would you remarry?'

"After a considerable period of grieving, I guess I would, I replied. We all need companionship.

"'Then,' she said, 'If I died and you remarried, would she live in this house?'

"Well, I said, we spent a lot of time getting this house the way we want it. I'm not ready to get rid of the house.

"'If I died and you remarried and she lived in this house, would she sleep in the same bed?' my wife asked.

"Well, the bed is almost new and it cost $2000 dollars. It's going to last a long time. I guess she would.

"'If I died and you remarried, and she lived in this house, and sleeps in our bed, would she use my golf clubs?' my wife asked.

"Oh no, I replied. She's left-handed."

Chapter Eight

Chronologically Challenged: Perils of Aging

First you forget names, then you forget faces, then you forget to pull your zipper up, then you forget to pull your zipper down.
—Leo Rosenberg (2003)

It's been said that life begins at 60—as does failing eyesight, painful arthritis, deeply etched wrinkles, diminished hearing, and the tendency to repeat stories three or four times to the same person. But, there are some benefits to attaining old age. If taken hostage, you will be among the first to be released. You can say, "When I was your age..." to more people. You don't have to worry about zits and pregnancy scares. Each year you experience less peer pressure. The older you are, the better you were. And best of all, if you are worried about losing you memory, just forget it.

The jokes and stories in this section deal with the developmental stage beyond mid-life, and put into bold relief the commonly-held stereotype that older people become absent-minded. Fortunately, and contrary to caricatures of the elderly, decline in mental acuity is not an inevitable consequence of the aging process.

Old age isn't for sissies, and—considering the alternative—aging is not so bad.

✳ ✳ ✳

Two elderly couples were enjoying friendly conversation when one of the men asked the other, "Fred, how was the memory clinic you went to last month?"

"Outstanding," Fred replied. "They taught us all the latest psychological techniques—visualization, association. It made a huge difference for me."

"That's great! What was the name of the clinic?"

Fred went blank. He thought and thought, but couldn't remember.

Then a smile broke across his face, and he asked, "What do you call that red flower with the long stem and thorns?"

"You mean a rose?"

"Yes, that's it!" He turned to his wife ... "Rose, what was the name of that clinic?"

* * *

An arrogant, self-made, 80-year-old man went to see a psychiatrist. "I've got an 18-year-old bride who's pregnant with my child. What do you think of that, 'eh, doc?"

"Well, let me tell you a story," said the psychiatrist. "I know a guy who is a great hunter, but one day he left home in a hurry and accidently picked up his umbrella instead of his rifle. Later that day, he came face to face with a huge grizzly bear. My friend raised his umbrella, pointed it at the bear, and squeezed the handle. And guess what? The bear dropped dead."

"That's impossible," said the patient. "Someone else must have shot that bear!"

"That's kind of what I'm getting at," said the psychiatrist.

* * *

An elderly lady, a bit confused, hesitated before leaving the clinic. A nurse, noting her confusion, inquired, "Have you vertigo?" She replied, "Yes, a mile."

* * *

Three elderly women were discussing the problems of growing old. One said, "Sometimes I find myself in front of the refrigerator with a jar of mayonnaise, and I can't remember if I am putting it away or making a sandwich."

Another said, "And I can trip on the stairs and not remember if I was walking up or down."

"Oh, well, I don't have those sort of problems, knock on wood," said the third, tapping her knuckles on the table, before adding, "That must be the door. I'll get it."

* * *

The young student nurse was puzzled why the aging professor needed three pairs of glasses. Finally she worked up courage to ask him.

He explained, "I have one pair for long sight, one pair for short sight, and the third pair to look for the other two."

* * *

An old man asked his wife to make him a hot fudge sundae. She went to the kitchen, and 20 minutes later came back with a plate of scrambled eggs instead. Seeing this, he flew into a rage and yelled, "Where's the bacon? I asked for bacon!"

* * *

A 95-year-old tycoon from Texas, diagnosed as bipolar, snuck out of the hospital and jetted to Tangier and bought himself a harem. The staff, very embarrassed, changed his diagnosis to "delusions of glandular."

* * *

An elderly widow and a widower had been dating for five years. He finally asked her to marry him, and she immediately said yes. But the next morning, he couldn't remember what her answer had been. In desperation, he decided to call her.

"This is really embarrassing," he began, "but when I asked you to marry me yesterday—well, this morning, I just couldn't remember what your answer was."

"Oh, I'm so glad you called," she said. "I remembered saying yes to someone, but I couldn't remember who it was!"

* * *

An elderly patient went to a therapist. "I need help. Do you remember me telling you about me hearing voices in my head? I've had them for years."

"Yes," nodded the therapist.

"Well, they suddenly stopped."

"That's great. So what's the problem?" asked the therapist.

"I think I'm going deaf," the man replied.

* * *

Three old gentlemen were at the psychologist's office for a memory test. The psychologist asked the first one, "What are two times two?" "194," was the reply.

The psychologist turned to the second old man. "What are two times two?"

"Thursday," replied the second old man.

Finally, the psychologist addressed the third old man. "What are two times two?"

"Four," came the answer.

"That's great," said the psychologist. "How did you get that?"

"Simple," said the third man, "I subtracted 194 from Thursday!"

* * *

The well-meaning social worker was seeing if Mrs. Englehardt qualified for admission to the local nursing home, and part of the standard procedure was a test for senility.

"And what's this?" she asked sweetly of the old German woman who was sitting at the dinner table.

"Dot? Dot's a spoon," answered Mrs. Englehardt.

"Very good," said the social worker. "And this?"

"Dot's a fork," answered the old woman.

"*Very* good. And this?" asked the social worker, holding up a knife.

"Dot's a phallic symbol."

* * *

"I went to see a new doctor last week," reported the client.

The therapist inquired, "How did it go?"

"Well," said the client, "the doctor said, 'That will be $50 in advance,' so I paid him and told him I had a terrible short-term memory."

"He said, 'That will be $50 in advance.'"

* * *

Client to therapist: "My brother's memory is as bad as mine. We both think we're an only child."

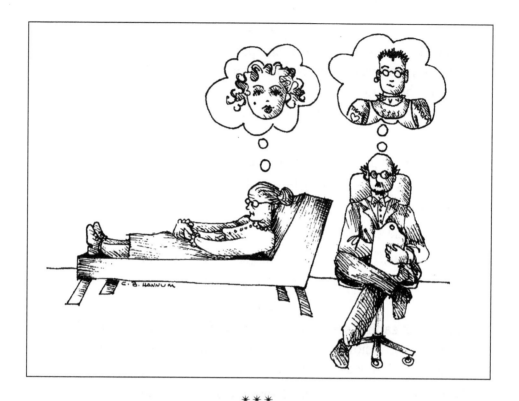

* * *

At his annual checkup, Horace was given an excellent bill of health.

"It must run in your family," commented the doctor. "How old was your dad when he died?"

"What makes you think he's dead?" asked Horace. "He's 90 and still going strong."

"Aha! And how long did your grandfather live?" asked the doctor.

"What makes you think he's dead, Doc? He's 106, and getting married to a 22-year-old next week," was the reply.

"At his age!" exclaimed the doctor. "Why does he want to marry such a young woman?"

"And what makes you think *he* wants to?"

* * *

At the counseling unit of a senior services center, Samuel was telling the counselor that he couldn't come in the next week.

"I'm getting married to a 19-year-old stripper," he said.

"Are you sure it's a good idea?" asked the counselor. "You're 75 years old. Having sex with a girl that young could be fatal."

Samuel shrugged, "If she dies, she dies."

* * *

An agitated patient was stomping around the therapist's office, running his hands through his hair, almost in tears.

"My memory's gone. Gone! I can't remember my wife's name ... can't remember my children's names ... can't remember what kind of car I drive ... can't remember where I work. It was all I could do to find my way here!"

"Calm down sir! How long have you been like this?" the therapist asked.

"Like what?" the patient responded.

* * *

Two elderly women were eating breakfast in a restaurant one morning. Ethel noticed something funny about Mabel's ear.

"Mabel, did you know you've got a suppository in your left ear?"

"I have a suppository?" asked Mabel, as she pulled it out and stared at it.

"Ethel, I'm glad you saw this thing. Now I think I now know where my hearing aid is."

* * *

A funeral service was being held for the elderly wife of a psychologist who was known to be a particularly nasty woman. At the end of the service, the pall bearers were carrying the casket out when they accidentally bumped into a wall, jarring the casket. They heard a faint moan! They opened up the casket and found that the woman was actually alive. She lived for ten more years, and then died.

Once again, a funeral was held; and at the end of it, the pall bearers were again carrying out the casket. As they carried the casket toward the door, the husband cried, "Watch that wall!"

* * *

A woman, recently widowed, was crying in a grief counselor's office.

"We were married 25 years before he died," she said dabbing away a tear.

"We never had an argument in all those years."

"Amazing," said the counselor, "how did you do it?"

"I outweighed him by forty pounds, and he was a coward."

* * *

Two elderly women were out driving in a large car. Both could barely see over the dashboard. As they were cruising along, they came to an intersection. The stoplight was red, but they just went on through. The woman in the passenger seat thought to herself, "I must be losing it. I could have sworn we just went through a red light."

After a few more minutes, they came to another intersection. The light was red again, and, again, they went right through.

This time the woman in the passenger seat was almost sure that the light had been red, but now she was really concerned that she was losing it. She was getting nervous and decided to pay very close attention to the road and the next intersection to see what was going on.

At the next intersection, sure enough, the light was definitely red, and they went right through. The friend turned to the other woman and said, "Mildred, did you know we just ran through three red lights in a row! You could have killed us!"

"OH CRAP," said Mildred. "Am I driving?"

* * *

A couple, both 78 years old, went to a counselor who specialized in sex therapy.

The therapist asked, "What can I do for you?" "We have some concerns about our love-making and wonder if you can help us," said the man.

"Sure," said the therapist. "I know this might be uncomfortable for you, but why don't you make love here in the office; and I will watch and then make some suggestions?"

When the couple finished, the therapist said that there was nothing wrong with the way they had intercourse and charged them $70.

The following week, the pair came in again with the same request. The therapist provided the same service and charged the same amount. This happened for several more weeks without variation.

Finally, the therapist asked, "What exactly is the problem you're having with intercourse?"

"Oh, we're not having a problem with intercourse," said the man. "She's married, and we can't go to her house. I'm married, and we can't go to my house. The Hilton charges $120. The Holiday Inn charges $110. We can do it here for $70 and I get $45 back from Medicare!"

* * *

Two elderly ladies had been friends for many decades. Over the years they had shared all kinds of activities and adventures. Lately, their activities had been limited to meeting a few times a week to play cards.

One day they were playing cards when one looked at the other and said, "Now don't get mad at me … I know we've been friends for a long time … but I just can't think of your name! I've thought and thought, but I can't remember it. Please tell me what you name is."

Her friend glared at her. For at least three minutes, she just stared and glared at her. Finally she said, "How soon do you need to know?"

* * *

Therapist: I understand you put your grandfather in a rest home.

Client: Well, not exactly. We didn't have the money so we just drove down the turnpike and put him in a rest area.

* * *

A social worker assigned to an outreach program is walking around a neighborhood, and she sees a gray-haired toothless old man sitting in a chair on his porch smiling serenely.

"I couldn't help but notice how happy you look," she says. "What's your secret for a long happy life?"

"I smoke three packs a day, drink a case of beer, eat fatty food, and never, ever exercise."

"Wow, that's amazing! How old are you?"

"I'm 26."

✳ ✳ ✳

An elderly man who was growing deaf finally bought an invisible hearing aid he saw advertized in the back of a magazine. "How do you like it?" asked his counselor. "Oh, I like it a great deal. I've heard sounds I didn't know existed."

"How does your family like it?" the counselor wondered. "Nobody in my family knows I have it. And I'm having a great time. I've changed my will three times."

✳ ✳ ✳

An elderly man told his psychologist, "I don't think my wife's hearing is as good as it use to be. What should I do?"

The psychologist replied, "Try this test first. When your wife is at the sink doing dishes, stand fifteen feet behind her and ask her a question. If she doesn't respond, keep moving closer, asking the same question until she hears you."

He went home and saw his wife preparing dinner. Standing fifteen feet behind her, he asked, "What's for dinner, honey?"

Hearing no reply, he moved up to ten feet behind her and repeated the same question. Still no reply, so he moved to five feet.

Still no answer.

Finally he stood directly behind her and said, "Honey, what's for dinner tonight?"

"FOR THE FOURTH TIME, I SAID CHICKEN, You'd better get your hearing checked."

✳ ✳ ✳

An eccentric old maid made an appointment with her lawyer to draw up her will. After the usual preliminaries of "sound mind" and all that, he asked just what she wanted in her will. "Well, I want to leave the bulk of my estate to my two cats Cuddles and Sweety."

"To your cats," repeated the lawyer as he applied pen to pad.

"Are you writing that down?" the elderly cat lover demanded.

"Not exactly," the attorney replied, "I'm just scratching out the part about sound mind."

* * *

My memory is not as sharp as it used to be. Also, my memory is not as sharp as it used to be.

* * *

A 70-year-old man goes to the doctor for a physical:

The doctor runs some tests and says to the man, "Well, everything seems to be in top condition physically, but what about spiritually? How is your connection with God?"

"Oh me and God are tight," says the man. "We have a real bond. He's good to me. Every night when I have to get up to go to the bathroom, he turns on the light for me, and when I leave he turns it back off."

Well, upon hearing this, the doctor was concerned and called the man's wife. "I'd like to speak to you about your husband's connection with God. He claims that every night when he goes to the bathroom God turns on the light for him and turns it off for him again when he leaves. Is this true?"

The wife shook her head. "That idiot, he's been peeing in the refrigerator!"

* * *

Rita was standing vigil over her husband's deathbed. As she held his hand, her warm tears ran silently down her face, splashed onto his face, and roused him from his slumber.

He looked up and his pale lips began to move slightly. "My darling," he whispered.

"Hush, my love," she said. "Go back to sleep. Shhh. Don't talk."

But he was insistent. "Rita," he said in his tired voice."I have to talk. I have something I must confess."

"There's nothing to confess," replied the weeping Rita. "It's all right. Everything's all right. Go to sleep now."

"No, no. I must die in peace, Rita. I slept with you sister, your best friend, and your mother."

Rita mustered a pained smile and stroked his hand. "Hush now dear, don't torment yourself. I know all about it," she said.

"Now you be still and let the poison work."

✳ ✳ ✳

John and Herbert, two elderly men, shared an apartment in a senior citizen complex. They agreed that the one who died first would make every effort to communicate with the other. John was the first one to die and for many months Herbert kept alert waiting to hear from him. Finally one night he awoke from a deep sleep and heard a familiar voice calling, "Herbert! Herbert!"

"John," cried Herbert "I can hear you! You've done it! Tell me, what's it like?"

"Well," said John," it's not bad; I'm in a very comfortable, quiet, dark place with flowers and trees all around. After enjoying sleep I come out and eat in beautiful green meadows. Then I have a little sex and go back to my dark comfort. After a lovely nap again I feel hungry, so I have more lovely green food to eat, and then a little sex, and then again back to sleep."

"Fantastic," said Herbert, "so that's what angels in Heaven do all day!"

"First, who said I'm an angel and second, who said I'm in Heaven?" replied John.

"I'm a rabbit in Kalamazoo, Michigan."

✳ ✳ ✳

My grandfather likes to take me aside and give me advice but he is a little forgetful. One day he took me aside and left me.

✳ ✳ ✳

A man of ninety who'd married a wisp of a girl in her early twenties was concerned about the marriage. His therapist, trying to be sensitive told him, "Be smart, and get a boarder."

The ninety-year-old man did as his therapist suggested. Several months later he returned for a session and proudly announced, "My wife is pregnant."

The therapist said, "Was I wrong in suggesting a boarder?"

"No," the man said, "but she's pregnant too!"

***

During a counseling group at a mental health clinic, the members were discussing the unforeseen possibility of their dying suddenly.

"We will all die some day, and none of us really knows when," observed the group leader. "Perhaps if we did we would do a better job in preparing ourselves."

Everybody nodded their heads in agreement with this remark.

Then the leader said to the group, "What would each of you do if you knew you had only four weeks to live?"

An older man said, "I would go out into my community and minister the Gospel to those that have not yet accepted the Lord into their lives."

Another man said, "I would spend all my time with my grandchildren and commit my life to getting to know them."

A woman responded, "I would spend the time with my husband knowing that he is unprepared to live alone."

Finally one of the more quiet members spoke, "I would go to my mother-in-law's house for the four weeks."

Everyone was puzzled by this answer, and the leader asked, "Why your mother-in-law's house?"

"Well," said the fellow slyly, "because that would be the longest four weeks of my life."

***

An elderly man had dinner at an upscale restaurant. After he finished his wine, he went to the restroom, and then walked out through the bar. Since it was a fine night, he decided to leave his car in the parking lot and walk home.

When he reached his front door he discovered he did not have his keys, which were in the pocket of his jacket, which he had left in the restroom. After he walked back to the restaurant and retrieved his jacket, he realized he had left his hat at the table, so he returned to the dining room.

When he reached his seat, his wife asked, "Is something wrong? You took such a long time in there."

* * *

An older fellow was celebrating his 100th birthday and everybody complemented him on how athletic and well-preserved he appeared. "Ladies and gentleman, I will tell you the secret of my success," he crackled. "I have been in the open air day after day for some 75 years now."

The celebrants were impressed and asked how he managed to keep up his rigorous fitness regime. "Well, you see, my wife and I were married 75 years ago. On our wedding night, we made a solemn pledge. Whenever we had a fight, the one who was proved wrong would go outside and take a walk."

* * *

An elderly man and woman, residents of a nursing home, sat in the day room talking. Feeling bored, the old woman says, "I'll bet you ten dollars I can guess your age." He is doubtful but agrees to the bet.

"Stand up, take off all your clothes, and turn around," she says. Now, he is even more skeptical, but he does exactly what she asks. Finally she announces, "You are eighty-seven-years old."

Astonished by her accuracy, he asks, "How can you tell?"

"Easy," she answered, "you told me yesterday."

* * *

The Senile Prayer

Grant me the senility to forget the people I never liked anyway, the good fortune to run into the ones I do, and the eyesight to tell the difference.

Chapter Nine

Temporary Sanity:
It's All in Your Head

If you talk to God you are praying; if God talks to you, you
have schizophrenia.
— Thomas Szasz (1973)

Affirmations are those positive statements that we repeat over and over in order to implant a desirable condition or intention into our minds. Repeating such statements as "I'm a good person" or "I'll not swear today" mobilizes inner resources for self-improvement. Over time, we are told, they strengthen who we are and reprogram our unconscious mind for a happier and more wholesome way of life.

So what happens when not-so-positive affirmations—those messages that are negative—sneak in? Most therapists would agree that the following self-talk, while perhaps reassuring, could use a bit of adjustment.

* * *

I assume full responsibility for my actions, except the ones that are someone else's fault.

* * *

My psychiatrist says I have an obsession with revenge. We'll see about that.

* * *

I need not suffer in silence, while I can still moan, whimper, and complain.

* * *

As I let go of my shoulds and feelings of guilt, I can get in touch with my Inner Sociopath.

* * *

In some cultures what I do would be considered normal.

* * *

I have the power to channel my imagination into ever-soaring levels of suspicion and paranoia.

* * *

I honor my personality flaws ... for without them, I would not have any personality at all.

* * *

Blessed are the flexible, for they can tie themselves into knots.

* * *

The next time the universe knocks at my door, I will pretend I'm not home.

* * *

Having control over myself is nearly as good as having control over others.

* * *

My intuition nearly makes up for my lack of good judgment.

* * *

Before I criticize a man, I'll walk a mile in his shoes—

In that way, if he gets angry, he's a mile away and in his bare feet.

* * *

I can change any thoughts that hurt into a reality that hurts even more.

* * *

Joan of Arc heard voices, too.

* * *

Therapy is expensive—popping bubble wrap is cheap.

* * *

Next mood swing: 6 minutes.

* * *

I am grateful that I am not as judgmental as all those censorious self-righteous people around me.

* * *

I respect the opinion of another; I just don't want to hear it.

* * *

As I learn the innermost secrets of the people around me, they reward me in many ways to keep me quiet.

* * *

When someone hurts me, forgiveness is cheaper than a lawsuit, but not nearly as gratifying.

* * *

The first step is to say nice things about myself and the second, to do nice things for myself. The third, to find me someone to buy me nice things.

* * *

All of me is beautiful and valuable—even the ugly, stupid, and disgusting parts.

* * *

Rehab. is for quitters.

* * *

I am at one with my duality.

* * *

I will strive to live each day as if it were my 50th birthday.

* * *

Only lack of imagination saves me from immobilizing myself with imaginary fears.

* * *

The only reason I would take up jogging is so I could hear heavy breathing again.

* * *

Today I will gladly share my experience and advice.

For there are no sweeter words than "I told you so."

* * *

To have a successful relationship, I must learn to make it look like I'm giving as much as I'm getting.

* * *

My mother is a travel agent for guilt trips.

* * *

I'm willing to make the mistakes, if someone else is willing to learn from them.

* * *

Growing old is mandatory; growing up is optional.

* * *

I am out of estrogen and I have a gun.

* * *

I finally got my head together, and my body fell apart.

* * *

My mind not only wanders, sometimes it leaves completely.

* * *

Insanity is my only means of relaxation.

* * *

Every time I think about exercise, I will lie down and the thought will go away.

* * *

God put me on earth to accomplish a certain number of things; and right now I am so far behind, I will never die.

* * *

Every day I beat my own previous record for number of consecutive days I've stayed alive.

* * *

There cannot be a crisis this week; my schedule is already full.

* * *

The nice thing about living in a small town is that when I don't know what I'm doing, someone else does.

* * *

If at first I don't succeed, I'll destroy all evidence that I tried.

* * *

For every action, there is an equal and opposite criticism.

* * *

The older I get, the tougher it is to lose weight.

My body and my fat are now really good friends.

* * *

False hope is nicer than no hope at all.

* * *

Just for today, I will not sit in my living room all day, in my underwear, watching TV.

I will move my TV into the bedroom.

* * *

Mondays are an awful way to spend 1/7th of my life.

* * *

The complete lack of evidence is the surest sign that the conspiracy is working.

* * *

Who can I blame for my own problems?

Give me just a minute ... I'll find someone.

* * *

Why should I waste my time reliving the past

when I can spend it worrying about the future?

* * *

I am learning that criticism is not nearly as effective as sabotage.

* * *

Becoming aware of my character defects leads me to the next step—blaming my parents.

* * *

The sooner I fall behind, the more time I'll have to catch up.

* * *

To understand all is to fear all.

* * *

I will find humor in everyday life by looking for people I can laugh at.

* * *

When life gives me lemons, I will make whiskey sours and go to bed.

* * *

Others are just jealous because the voices talk to me.

* * *

I don't have an attitude problem; they have a perception problem.

* * *

I use to be schizophrenic, but now we are better.

* * *

It's as bad as you think, and they ARE out to GET you.

* * *

Why is the alphabet in that order?

Is it because of that song?

* * *

Friends help you move ... Real friends help you move bodies.

* * *

I do whatever my Rice Krispies tell me to do.

* * *

P.M.S.?! Hell, this is one of my better days.

* * *

There are three kinds of people in the world: those who can count and those who can't.

* * *

I said "no" to drugs but they wouldn't listen.

* * *

I feel more affirmed in knowing that two in every one person is a schizophrenic.

* * *

Sometimes I stop to think and forget to start again.

* * *

If someone with a multiple personality threatens to kill herself, is it considered a hostage situation?

* * *

My panic attacks are a cause for alarm.

* * *

With my delusions of grandeur, I'm never down and out.

* * *

I bet you a hundred dollars I can quit gambling.

* * *

With my multiple personality disorder, there's always a full house.

* * *

I'm not myself today. Maybe I'm you.

* * *

My inferiority complex is not as good as yours.

* * *

My indecision is final.

* * *

I had to give up masochism. I was enjoying it too much.

* * *

I don't suffer insanity, I enjoy every minute of it.

* * *

Aim low ... reach your goals ... avoid disappointment.

* * *

My fear is that life may have no meaning—or worse, it may have meaning for which I disapprove.

* * *

It's been lovely, but I have to scream now.

* * *

There's no problem so big or complicated that it can't be run away from.

* * *

Consciousness is that annoying time between naps.

* * *

Give me ambiguity or give me something else.

* * *

I've always been a hypochondriac. As a little boy, I'd eat my M & M's one by one with a glass of water.

* * *

Hypochondria is the only illness I don't have.

* * *

The best cure for hypochondria is to forget about your own body and get interested in somebody else's.

* * *

As I learn to trust the universe, I no longer need to carry a gun.

* * *

Being a man in a lesbian body sucks.

* * *

Madness takes its toll. Please have the exact change.

* * *

If you can't change your mind, are you sure you have one?

* * *

I don't suffer stress, I'm a carrier.

* * *

Heredity runs in our family.

* * *

They told me I was crazy … but what do Cheerios know?

* * *

Don't worry if you're a kleptomaniac; you can take something for it.

* * *

Kleptomaniacs are people who help themselves because they can't help themselves.

* * *

Paranoids are people, too. They have their own problems.

It's easy to criticize; but if everyone hated you, you would be paranoid, too.

* * *

Once I had multiple personalities, but now we are feeling well.

* * *

Just because you are paranoid, doesn't mean they aren't out to get you.

* * *

I no longer need to punish, deceive or compromise myself—unless of course, I want to stay employed.

* * *

If I knew why I was so anxious I wouldn't need to be so anxious.

* * *

The difference between sex and death is with death—no one makes fun of you.

* * *

I always tell the truth even if I have to lie to do it.

* * *

I'm glad I'm not bisexual. I couldn't stand to be rejected by men as well as women.

* * *

Just give me chocolate and no one will get hurt.

* * *

I was going to buy a copy of *The Power of Positive Thinking* and then I thought what the hell good would that do?

* * *

Marriage is not a word, it's a sentence.

* * *

There's nothing wrong with the average person that a good psychiatrist can't exaggerate.

* * *

I quit therapy because my analyst was trying to help me behind my back.

* * *

I asked my shrink to show me one positive result from all my visits. He showed me his new Porsche.

* * *

My opinions may have changed, but not the fact that I am right.

* * *

Even paranoids have real enemies.

* * *

It's hard to be nice to some paranoid schizophrenic just because she lives in your body.

* * *

I ain't going to no stinken shrink. I'm small enough already.

* * *

Reality is for the little people.

* * *

If God wanted us to go naked, we would have been born that way.

* * *

Blessed are the pure for they shall inhibit the earth.

* * *

There is only one cure for snoring, insomnia.

* * *

I was going to have an audience with the Pope, but when I offered to give him one, he turned me down.

* * *

I hate myself for thinking I'm better than others. Why can't I have delusions like everybody else?

* * *

I was born prematurely—I'm fifty years ahead of my time.

* * *

So what if I am fat—nature just overdid a good thing.

* * *

Of course others don't think I'm as smart as I do—but then they don't have brains to realize it.

* * *

People find me shocking because I have so much electricity coursing through my brain.

* * *

I wouldn't say I'm a genius. Why state the obvious.

* * *

My motto is "Never admit to anything." But I don't always stick to it. I do admit I'm a genius.

* * *

My egotism doesn't keep me from seeing reality. In fact, it's my seeing reality that made me egotistical.

* * *

I was a precocious child. When only twelve I asked my mother, "Is God made in my image?"

* * *

I'm not very much, but I'm all that I think about.

* * *

I am far too righteous to ever be sanctimonious.

* * *

I'd go to a psychiatrist but I don't really think I could help him.

* * *

Sometimes I act pretty stupid, just so people will accept me as an equal.

* * *

Sex is my religion ... let us pray.

* * *

Support mental health, or I'll kill you.

MEDITATIONS

My therapist said the way to achieve inner peace is to complete all of the things we have started but have never finished.

So I looked around my house to see all the things I started and hadn't finished—and before leaving the house this morning, I finished off a bottle of Merlot, a bottle of White Zinfandel, a bottle of Bailey's Irish Cream, a bottle of Kahlua, a package of Oreos, the remainder of my old Prozac prescription, the rest of the cheesecake, some Dorritos, and a box of chocolates.

You have no idea how frigging good I feel.

* * *

Picture yourself by a stream.

Birds are singing in the cool, crisp mountain air.

Nothing can bother you.

No one knows this sacred place.

You are in total seclusion from the world.

The soothing sound of a gentle waterfall fills the air with a cascade of serenity.

The water is clear.

You can easily make out the face of a person whose head you're holding under the water.

There now, feeling better?

* * *

PRAYERS

So Far, So Good

Dear Lord,

So far today, I'm doing all right.

I have not gossiped, lost my temper, and been greedy, grumpy, nasty, selfish, or self-indulgent.

I have not whined, complained, cursed, or eaten any chocolate.

I have charged nothing on my credit card.

But I will be getting out of bed in a minute, and I think that I will really need your help then.

Amen

* * *

Who Me—Control?

Dear Lord,

Help me to relax about insignificant details, beginning tomorrow at 7:41:23 EST.

God help me to consider people's feelings, even if most of them ARE hypersensitive.

God help me to take responsibility for my own actions, even though they are usually NOT my fault.

God, help me try not to RUN everything, but if you need some help, please feel free to ASK ME!

Lord, help me to be more laid back, and help me to do it EXACTLY RIGHT.

God help me to take things more seriously, especially laughter, parties & dancing.

God give me patience, and I mean Now, Lord, help me not be a perfectionist. (Did I write that correctly?) God help me to finish everything that I sta ...

A ...

* * *

Sanity and Other Good Things

Now I lay me down to sleep,

I pray my sanity to keep.

For if some peace I do not find,

I'm pretty sure I'll lose my mind.

I pray I find a little quiet.

Far from the daily family riot.

May I lie back and not have to think

about what they're stuffing down the sink,

or who they're with, or where they're at,
and what they're doing to the cat.
I pray for time all to myself
(did something just fall off a shelf?)
To cuddle in my nice, soft bed
(Oh no, another goldfish—dead!)
Some silent moments for goodness sake
(Did I just hear a window break?)
And that I need not cook or clean—
(well, heck, I've got the right to dream.)
Yes now I lay me down to sleep,
I pray my wits about me keep,
But as I look around I know—
I must have lost them long ago!
Amen

Chapter Ten

You Gotta Be Crazy to Be Here: Hospital Madness

An asylum for the sane would be empty in America.
—George Bernard Shaw (2000)

Modern psychiatric hospitals, once called *asylums,* are a far cry from what they were in the not-so-good old days. Typically, *inmates* lived in squalid surroundings with little or no treatment. With the advent of psychotropic drugs, and more sophisticated forms of treatment, folks now spend less time in the hospital and return to their communities to live more functional and productive lives.

One thing has not changed, and that's the chronic institutional absurdity common to large institutions. And here lies a paradox. The hospitals, characterized by the exaggeration of routine, fragmented communication, reality confusion, and resistance to change, begin to resemble the patients they serve. And, no surprise, the patients begin to bear a striking resemblance to the therapeutic system that's there to heal them.

The following humor, full of parody, satire, hyperbole, and incongruity, reflects what patients and staff have always suspected—psychiatric hospitals can be downright crazy-making.

* * *

How do you tell the difference between the staff and the patients at a psychiatric hospital?

The patients get better and leave.

* * *

I was thrown out of a mental hospital for depressing the other patients.

—Attributed to Oscar Levant (2005)

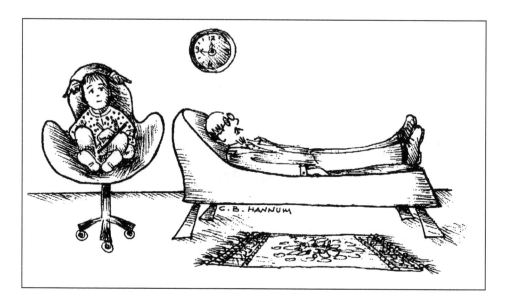

* * *

During a visit to the psychiatric hospital, a visitor asked the medical director what was the criteria which defined whether or not a patient should be institutionalized.

"Well," said the director, "we fill up a bath tub, then we offer a teaspoon, a teacup and a bucket to the patient and ask him or her to empty the bathtub."

"Oh, I understand," said the visitor. "A normal person would use the bucket because it's better than the spoon or the teacup."

"No," said the director, "a normal person would pull the plug. Do you want a bed near the window?"

* * *

Nurse: I'm afraid you are mentally ill.

Patient: Well, are *you* all right?

Nurse: Certainly, I'm all right.

Patient: Then I'm glad *I'm* mentally ill.

* * *

How can you tell the therapists on a psychiatric ward from the patients?

The patients take their medication.

* * *

A farmer was driving past a psychiatric hospital with a load of fertilizer.

A patient saw him and called out, "What are you hauling?"

"Fertilizer," said the farmer.

"What are you going to do with it?" was the next question.

"Put it on strawberries," was the answer.

"You ought to live in here," said the patient. "We get sugar and cream on them."

* * *

Nowadays we don't treat mental illness by sending people to the madhouse.

We charge $120 an hour and send them to the poorhouse!

* * *

How do you tell the difference between the staff and the patients at a psychiatric hospital?

Not every one of the patients thinks he is God.

* * *

The nurse who can smile when things go wrong is probably going off duty.

* * *

A patient in a hospital sat near the front door patiently holding a fishing pole and a line.

"What are you fishing for?" asked a visitor.

"Suckers," he said without looking up.

"Caught any?"

"You're the ninth!"

* * *

How do you tell the difference between the staff and the patients at a psychiatric hospital?

The staff has the keys!

* * *

A man is strolling past the psychiatric hospital and suddenly remembers an important meeting. Unfortunately, his watch has stopped and he cannot tell if he is late or not. Then he notices a patient similarly strolling about within the hospital fence. Calling out to the patient, the man says, "Pardon me, sir, but do you have the time?"

The patient calls back, "One moment!" and throws himself upon the ground, pulling out a short stick as he does. He pushes the stick into the ground and pulling out a carpenter's level, assures himself that the stick is vertical.

With a compass, the patient locates north and, with a steel ruler, measures the precise length of the shadow cast by the stick.

Withdrawing a slide rule from his pocket, the patient calculates rapidly, then swiftly packs up all his tools and turns back to the pedestrian saying, "It is now precisely 3:29 pm, provided today is August 16, which I believe it is."

The man can't help but be impressed by this demonstration and sets his watch accordingly.

Before he leaves, he says to the patient, "That was really quite remarkable. But tell me what you do on a cloudy day or at night when the stick casts no shadow?"

The patient holds up his wrist and says, "I just look at my watch."

* * *

A fellow walks past a wooden fence at a psychiatric hospital, and he hears the patients inside chanting, "Thirteen, Thirteen, Thirteen!"

Quite curious about this, he finds a hole in the fence and looks in.

Someone inside the fence pokes him in the eye.

Then everyone inside the fence starts chanting, "Fourteen, Fourteen, Fourteen!"

* * *

Overheard in group therapy:

"I can't help it. I keep thinking my inferiority complex is bigger and better than everybody else's."

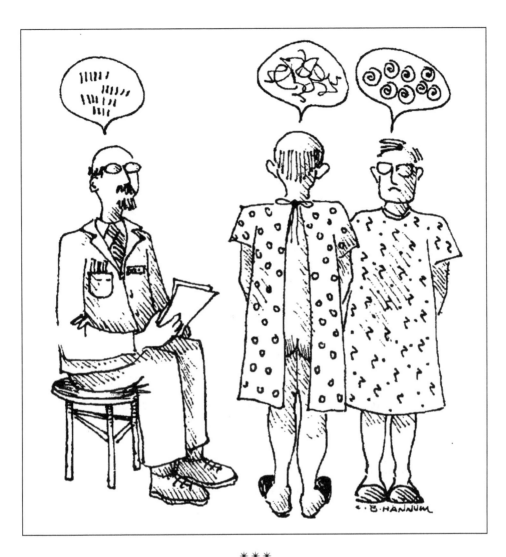

* * *

Patient: Bill over there talks to himself. That shows he's insane.

Nurse: Ridiculous. You wouldn't be insane just because you talk to yourself.

Patient: No?

Nurse: Of course not, I talk to myself. Do you think I'm insane?

Patient: I wouldn't say you're insane *if* you talked to yourself. But you *would* be if you listened.

* * *

Psychiatric hospitals today have highly advanced techniques, like giving patients shock therapy. The bill!

* * *

"The hospital really helped me a lot," said the young woman. "I wouldn't answer the phone because I was afraid. Now I answer it whether it rings or not."

* * *

A newspaper was running a competition to discover the most high-principled, sober, well behaved local citizen. Among the entries came one which read:

"I don't smoke, touch intoxicants or gamble. I am faithful to my wife and never look at another woman. I am hard working, quiet and obedient. I never go to movies or the theater and I go to bed early every night and rise with the dawn. I attend chapel regularly without fail.

I've been like this for the past three years. But just wait until next spring, when they let me out of here!"

* * *

Doctor: I think you're suffering from paranoia, so I'm referring you to a psychiatric hospital.

Patient: HA! You're only doing that because you hate having me as a patient.

* * *

A bishop visiting a psychiatric hospital was told by his guide that one of the patients insisted he was God. The bishop expressed interest in meeting the man who proved to be a venerable and dignified figure with a flowing white beard.

"I understand you are God," said the bishop.

"That's correct," replied the old man with a gentle bow.

"Well, there is one thing I would like very much to know. When you speak in the Bible of creating the world in six days, do you mean this literally or metaphorically? Do you mean six days of twenty-four hours each, or do you mean eons, or ages?"

"I am sorry," replied the old fellow, "but I make it a practice to never talk shop."

* * *

One of the patients of a hospital fancied himself to be a painter, and, with the help of his understanding doctor, was given a room for a studio and supplied with the necessary paints, brushes, and easel.

After a time, it was suggested that a visiting art therapist plus hospital staff come to the unveiling of a just completed masterpiece. With a flourish, the painter pointed to the obviously untouched piece of canvas, mounted on an easel.

"How do you like it?" asked the proud artist.

"Fine," said the art therapist. "But what is it?"

"It represents the passage of the Children of Israel through the Red Sea."

"But, where is the sea?"

"It's been driven back as related in the Bible."

"And where are the Israelites?" he asked.

"They have already crossed over."

"What about the pursuing Egyptians—where are they?"

"They haven't yet arrived," explained the artist.

*　*　*

A first-year psychiatric resident at a Veteran's Administration Hospital was attempting to get to know the patients to which he was assigned. One morning he met a patient playing solitaire in the day room. After introducing himself, he asked the patient how he came to be in the hospital.

"Well sir, you see I married a widow with a grown-up daughter, and then my father married my wife's daughter. That made my wife the mother-in-law of her father-in-law, and my brother became my step-son. Then my stepmother, the daughter of my wife, had a son and that boy, of course, was my brother, because he was my father's son; but he was also my wife's stepson, and therefore, her grandson, and that made me the grandfather of my stepbrother. Then my wife had a son, so my mother-in-law, the stepsister of my son, is also his grandmother be-cause his stepsister is his wife. I am the brother of my own son, who is also the son of my step-grandmother. I am my mother's brother-in-law, my wife is her own child's aunt, my son is my father's nephew, and I am my own grandfather. That's one of the reasons I am here, sir."

* * *

Nurse: We have two dinners today—hamburger or fish. Take your pick.

Patient: No thanks, I'll take my hammer.

* * *

A clergyman had occasion to preach to patients in a hospital. During one of his long and tedious sermons, he noticed that one of the patients paid the closest attention, his eyes riveted upon the preacher's face. Such interest was most flattering. After the service, the speaker observed that the man spoke to the superintendent as soon as he possibly could.

"Didn't that man speak to you about my sermon?"

"Yes."

The superintendent tried to sidestep, but the preacher insisted.

"Well," the superintendent said at last, "what the man said was, 'Just think, he's out, and I'm in.'"

* * *

A man visiting a psychiatric hospital observed a fellow in a small room who was constantly calling, "Susie, oh Susie, come back to me."

The visitor did not pay much attention to the poor fellow but continued his walk through the halls of the building. Presently he came to another patient who was physically shaking and appeared scared to death. Over and over, the man muttered, "Don't let Susie in here. Keep Susie away from me."

The man began to wonder if there was a connection and asked the nurse, "What's the meaning of this Susie business?"

"Well," replied the nurse, "Susie was the sweetheart of the first guy. He was going away to college and asked Susie to marry him. When he came home a month later, he found out that Susie had married someone else. He couldn't overcome his grief, and what you see is the result."

As the guide began to walk away, the man stopped her. "But, what about the man who looks so frightened?" he asked.

"Oh," said the nurse, "I thought you understood, that's the fellow who married Susie."

* * *

"Who are you?" asked the hospital patient.

"I'm the new medical director."

"Well, it won't take long for them to knock that notion out of your head. I was Napoleon when I came here."

* * *

A very loud and arrogant minister was conducting Sunday services in the hospital. His discourse was suddenly interrupted by one of the patients crying out widely, "Do we have to listen to this rubbish?"

The minister, surprised and confused, turned to the nurse and asked, "Should I stop speaking?"

"No, no," replied the nurse, "keep right on going. His outburst won't happen again. That man has only one sane moment every seven years."

* * *

A woman visiting a hospital became intrigued with an elderly gentleman standing near the nursing station.

"And, how long have you been here?" she inquired.

"Twelve years," was the answer.

"Do they treat you well?"

"Yes."

After addressing a few more questions to him, the visitor passed on. She noticed that the nurse who was escorting her was giggling. When asked the reason for her mirth, the nurse told her that the older man was none other than the hospital's medical director. Embarrassed, the visitor hurried back to make her apologies.

How successful she was may be gathered from her words.

"I'm sorry doctor; I'll never be governed by appearances again."

* * *

The pilot of the plane began to laugh uncontrollably. He laughed and laughed and laughed. Finally, a curious passenger went forward and asked him why he was laughing.

"Oh, I've been thinking of all the excitement at the psychiatric hospital when they find out I've escaped."

* * *

Therapist: You'll never leave the hospital until you get over these phobias.

Patient: I was afraid you'd say that.

* * *

"Dear me," said the lady to the Medical Director of the hospital, "what a vicious looking woman we just passed in the corridor. Is she dangerous?"

"She is at times," replied the Medical Director evasively.

"But why do you allow her such freedom?"

"Can't help it."

"But she's a patient and under your control."

"No, she's neither under my control nor a patient. She's my wife."

* * *

A man who had been hospitalized for some years finally seemed to have improved to the point where it was thought he might be released.

The hospital superintendent, in a fit of commendable caution, decided to interview him.

"Tell me," he said, "if we release you as we are considering, what do you intend to do with your life?"

The patient said, "It would be wonderful to get back to real life; and, if I do, I will certainly refrain from making my former mistake. I was a nuclear physicist, you know; and it was the stress of my work in weapons research that helped put me here. If I am released, I shall confine myself to work in pure theory, where I trust the situation will be less difficult and stressful."

"Marvelous," said the superintendent.

"Or else," the patient ruminated, "I might teach. There is something to be said for spending one's life in bringing up a new generation of scientists."

"Absolutely," said the superintendent.

"Then again, I might write. There is considerable need for books on science for the general public. Or I might even write a novel based on my experiences in this fine institution."

"An interesting possibility," responded the superintendent.

"And finally, if none of these things appeals to me, I can always continue to be a micro-wave."

* * *

Student Nurse: Why do the patients call that man Jigsaw?

Supervisor: Every time he's faced with a problem, he goes to pieces.

* * *

One Sunday morning a group of patients at a psychiatric hospital in Michigan were being shepherded to the Catholic and Protestant chapels. One patient did not enter either chapel but continued walking toward the main gate.

When the nursing staff caught up with him and asked where he was going the patient replied, "I was told I could go to the church of my choice and that's in California."

* * *

Patient: I'm a failure!

Nurse: You don't feel good about yourself. Why don't you try the power of positive thinking?

Patient: All right—I'm positive I'm a failure!

* * *

A well known politician asked his friend, a professor of speech, for some advice on presenting interesting speeches. The professor suggested, "You should start with a question like, 'Why are we all here?'"

The politician tried out the idea before various audiences and it went well. Well that is until he somehow got persuaded to speak to patients in a psychiatric hospital. He began his usual way, "Why are we all here?"

Quick as a flash came back a reply from a voice in the audience, "Because we aren't all there."

* * *

A patient in a psychiatric unit advises a new patient:

"If someone ever catches you talking to yourself, the best thing to do is point at a chair and say, 'He started it.' That way they won't think you're crazy."

* * *

New patient: Can your hospital cure me of compulsive lying?

Intake worker: If you have enough money to afford the expensive treatment.

Patient: No problem, I just won the lottery yesterday.

* * *

Overheard in a hospital team meeting:

"I think the number-one problem in this hospital is that nobody wants to take responsibility for anything.

But don't quote me."

* * *

Psychiatrists have evolved from doing psychotherapy with patients to primarily writing prescriptions. In sum, psychiatry had been reduced to three words: ill, pill, and bill.

* * *

A visitor to Houston asked, "What's the fastest way to a nearby psychiatric hospital?"

A local told him, "Say something bad about Texas!"

* * *

A nurse walks over to a patient sitting in the hospital's day room. "Congratulations, Mr. Kemp. Our team of doctors and therapist thinks you're well enough to see your bill."

* * *

Patient runs into another patient in a psychiatric unit.

"Gee Bill, you look very stressed."

"Stressed? You're kidding. Look how slowly I'm twitching."

* * *

Homer, a patient diagnosed as having an anti-social personality disorder, was hospitalized in a tightly-secured forensic facility. One day he received a letter from his wife living in rural Maine.

"Darling, there is not an able-bodied person around to help me with the chores. The garden is in ruin, and I am going to have to dig it up myself."

In the return mail Homer wrote, "Don't dig up the garden. That's where the guns are buried."

A week later his wife replied, "Your letter must have been censored. The police were here and dug up every square foot of the garden."

Homer wrote back, "Plant vegetables."

* * *

The limousine pulled up in front of the psychiatric hospital, and the aristocratic looking gentleman got out. "Is this an asylum for the insane?" he asked an attendant.

"Yes sir," said the attendant.

"Do they accept inmates upon their own recommendations?"

"Why do you ask?"

"Well you see, I've just gotten hold of a package of my old love letters and ..."

* * *

Why are therapists never committed to a psychiatric hospital?

How do you tell when they go crazy?

* * *

Q. What's the difference between a psychiatric hospital and a college?

A. In the mental hospital, you must show improvement to get out.

* * *

A legislative committee was assigned to investigate conditions in a mental hospital in Illinois. There was a dance the evening of the day the committee arrived, and members were invited to attend.

During the course of the dance, a legislative member asked a pretty patient to dance. "I don't remember having seen you before," she inquired. "How long have you been a patient here?"

"Oh, I'm not a patient," said the legislator. "I'm a member of a special legislative committee which came over here today from Springfield to investigate the hospital."

"Of course," responded the lady patient. "How stupid of me. I knew the moment I saw you, you were either a member of the legislature or a patient, and for the life of me I couldn't figure out which."

✳ ✳ ✳

Two outpatient therapists were discussing a patient:

"I don't think we can hospitalize her. On the other hand, if she were already in, I don't think she would get out."

✳ ✳ ✳

A private psychiatric hospital that prides itself on creative milieu therapy recently held its annual softball game between the professional staff and the patients.

The psychiatrist, psychologist and social workers whipped the patient team something terrible. Unhappy with the outcome, the patients chose not to let the loss go without a face-saving response.

The following memo was posted on the hospital bulletin board for all to see.

The patients are pleased to announce that for this year's softball season we came in second place, having lost but one game all year. The professional staff, however, had a rather dismal year as they won only one game.

Chapter Eleven

Oedipal Wrecks:
The Mad Psychoanalysts

I'm going to give my psychoanalyst one more year, then
I'm going to Lourdes.
—Woody Allen (1997)

A whimsical stereotype of psychotherapy, often found in cartoons and outdated joke books, is a psychoanalyst's office with a woman lying on a couch. Sitting behind her taking copious notes is the analyst—a bald, bespectacled man resembling Sigmund Freud. During her three-to-four sessions per week, he analyzes her dreams, unhappy childhood, anger at her mother, penis-envy, and an under- or over-charged libido.

While still practiced, psychoanalysis is no longer fashionable as it once was. Folks just don't have the financial resources or the time to spend in long-term therapy. And, most therapists avoid psychic-archeology preferring instead briefer therapies where they have face-to-face interaction with their clients.

Modern psychotherapists who have a couch in their office use it primarily for family counseling or for taking a quick nap after lunch. The following jokes, some from the 1930's, characterize the traditional couch and dream routine.

* * *

Psychiatrist to Internal Revenue agent on couch: "Nonsense! The whole world isn't against you—the people of the United States, perhaps, but not the whole world."

* * *

How many Freudian psychoanalysts does it take to change a light bulb?

Two. One to change the bulb and one to hold the penis ... I mean ladder.

* * *

"Isn't that nice?" said the therapist. "They just appointed a resident psychoanalyst for Yellowstone National Park. No couch: Sleeping bags."

* * *

During the past four years, Joe had been seeing a psychoanalyst for fear that he had monsters under his bed. It had been years since he had gotten a good night's sleep. Furthermore, his progress had been very poor and he knew it. So, one day out of frustration, he stopped seeing the psychoanalyst and decided to try something different.

A few weeks later, Joe met his old psychoanalyst in the supermarket. Much to the therapist's surprise, Joe looked well-rested, energetic, and cheerful. "Doc!" Joe says, "It's amazing! I'm cured!"

"That's great news!" says the psychoanalyst. "You seem to be doing much better. How come?"

"I went to see another doctor," Joe says enthusiastically, "and he cured me in just ONE session!"

"One?" the psychoanalyst asked incredulously.

"Yeah," continued Joe, "my new doctor is a behaviorist."

"A behaviorist?" the psychoanalyst asks."How did he cure you in one session?"

"Oh, easy," says Joe. "He told me to cut the legs off my bed."

* * *

She had been seeing the psychoanalyst for years, pouring out her heart to him twice a week. However, she was making no progress and the doctor didn't believe she ever would.

"Mrs. Porter," he said at the end of one session, "do you think these sessions are doing you any good?"

"Not really," she said. "My inferiority complex is a strong as ever."

"Mrs. Porter," the doctor said, "I have something to tell you. You don't have an inferiority complex. You are, in fact, inferior."

* * *

Why is psychoanalysis a lot quicker for a man than for a woman?

Because, when it's time to go back to childhood, a man is already there.

* * *

There was a woman so pathologically tidy that her doctor sent her to a psychoanalyst.

But it was a complete waste of time. She spent the first four sessions rearranging the couch.

* * *

A man came into the analyst's office, lay down on the couch and told the doctor he needed help ridding his mind of an obsession. "All I can think of day and night is making love to a horse. It's driving me nuts."

"I see," said the therapist, rubbing his goatee. "Now would that be to a stallion or to a mare?"

"A mare, of course," retorted the patient, pulling himself upright indignantly. "What do you think I am a pervert or something?"

* * *

Two psychoanalysts meet for drinks, and one says to the other, "I thought I had been completely analyzed, but yesterday I experienced the most remarkable Freudian slip."

The friend nods and waits to hear more.

The first psychoanalyst goes on, "I was having dinner with my mother, and I meant to say, 'please pass the butter.'" But instead I said, "you miserable bitch you ruined my life."

* * *

The analyst thought it was very presumptuous of the patient to lie down on the couch while waiting for him.

Fighting back his anger he asked sarcastically, "Are you tired?"

"No."

"Then why are you lying down?"

"In case I get tired."

* * *

A young woman went to consult a psychoanalyst. On entering the examining room she was asked to lie down on the couch.

"No thanks, Doctor, that's how my problems began."

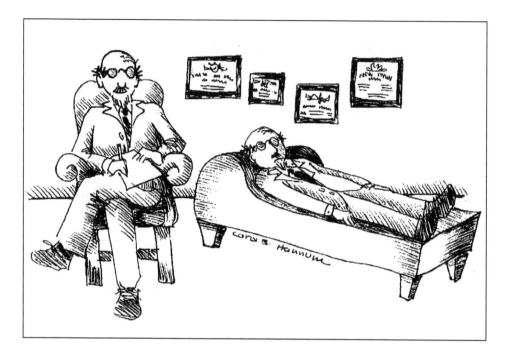

* * *

A young man was running around with too many women, so the
father decided to send him to the leading psychoanalyst in New York
City. It was a long drawn-out analysis, and the bill was very high; but
the father felt it was worth it if a cure was reached. Finally, when the
son returned, he demanded to know what had been covered in treatment.

"Did you tell the doctor how we caught you with the maid when
you were ten?"

The son nodded.

"Did you tell him we couldn't keep a cook for the last ten years
because of you? Twenty-three cooks we ran through."

The son nodded.

"Did you tell him about the five models, the 33 college girls, and
what happened to the superintendent's wife?"

He nodded again.

"So tell me," says the father. "What did the doctor say?"

"He said I have homosexual tendencies."

* * *

The man appeared at his analyst's office in a frenzied state. "I dreamed I was among three hundred dancing girls. There were luscious blondes, brunettes, and redheads, all buxomly, leggy, beautiful. It was terrible."

The analyst asked, "Why terrible?"

"I was the third girl from the end," the man replied.

* * *

The man lay on the couch telling his analyst a sad tale. "I see my brother," he said. "And he is walking down a long corridor, walking up 13 steps into a green door. There are lots of people standing around. They're covering his eyes. Ooh, Doctor, what does it mean?"

"Well," said the analyst, "if they ain't playing blind man's bluff, he's in real trouble."

* * *

A woman goes to see a psychoanalyst:

"You've got to help me," she said. "My husband thinks he's a race horse. He neighs, sleeps on straw, and even eats oats."

The analyst thinks for a moment. "No problem. I can help him, but it will be expensive."

"Oh, money is no problem," says the wife. "He's already won two races."

* * *

One woman to another:

"I must say that after three years of analysis, my husband is not so fussy about having the yolks right in the middle of his fried eggs anymore."

* * *

A client enters an analyst's office and sees an old friend.

Client: Are you coming or going?

Friend: If I knew whether I was coming or going, I wouldn't be here.

* * *

A fellow who lived with his mother celebrated his 40th birthday and the completion of his psychoanalysis on the same day. To celebrate the two occasions, the doting mother prepared an elaborate dinner.

At the close of the meal, she presented her son with two ties, one blue and the other red. As he put on the red tie, his mother's eyes filled with tears and she asked, "What's the matter dear, don't you like the blue one?"

* * *

Two old friends, lunching together for the first time in months, discovered that they were being analyzed by the same psychoanalyst. "Let's give him a problem that really will floor him," proposed one.

"I have an idea," said the other. "We'll make up an elaborate dream with all kinds of interesting ramifications that I'll describe in my morning session with him. You tell him the same dream when you hit the couch in the afternoon."

With fiendish glee, the conspirators perfected their plot; and, as planned, the first patient reeled off the gory details the following morning while the analyst filled his pad.

At 4:30 pm, the second patient gave an identical report.

The analyst said not one word until the recital was complete. Then he slapped his pencil and pad down and jumped from his chair. "This is the most remarkable coincidence in my professional career."

"What's the problem?" asked his tormentor, tongue in cheek.

"You won't believe this is possible, but you're the third patient who has had this exact dream in the past 24 hours."

* * *

"Mr. Bowman," the analyst said, "I think this will be your last visit."

"Does this mean I'm cured?" he asked.

"For all practice purposes, yes," she said. "I think we can safely say that your kleptomania is now under control. You haven't stolen anything in two years, and you seem to know where the kleptomania comes from."

"Well, that's terrific, Doctor. Before I go, I'd like to tell you something. Although our relationship is strictly professional, it's been one of the most rewarding of my life. I wish I could do something to repay you for helping me."

"You paid my fee," the analyst said. "That's the only responsibility you have."

"I know," Bowman said. "But isn't there some personal favor I could do for you?"

"Well," said the analyst, "I'll tell you what. If you ever suffer a relapse, my son could use a nice flat screen television."

* * *

A sad looking man went to an analyst:

"I've lost all desire to go on. Life has become too hectic, too confused."

"Yes," said the therapist chuckling sympathetically. "I understand. We all have our problems. You'll need a year or two of treatment, twice a week at $120.00 a session."

There was a pause. "Well, that solves your problems, Doc. Now, how about mine?"

* * *

"Mrs. Smith," the analyst said, "you're all better now and your treatment is over."

"Oh doctor, I can't believe it. Is there something I can do for you in return for all these years?"

"You have paid your bill and that's all I require."

"But doctor, that isn't enough. You're incredible. I could hug and kiss you."

"Please don't do that. Actually, we shouldn't even be lying here on the couch together."

* * *

All psychoanalysts are psychological, but some are more psycho than logical.

* * *

A man walked into a bar and ordered a glass of white wine. He took a sip of the wine, and then tossed the remainder into the bartender's face. Before the bartender could recover from the surprise, the man began weeping.

"I'm sorry," he said, "I'm really sorry. I keep doing this to bartenders. I can't tell you how embarrassing it is to have a compulsion like this."

Far from being angry, the bartender was sympathetic. Before long, the bartender was suggesting that the man see an analyst about his problem.

"I happen to have the name of a psychoanalyst," the bartender said. "My brother and my wife have both been treated by him, and they say he's as good as they come."

The man wrote down the name of the doctor, thanked the bartender, and left. The bartender smiled, knowing he'd done a good deed for a fellow human being.

Six months later, the man was back. "Did you do what I suggested?" the bartender asked serving the glass of wine.

"I certainly did," the man said. "I've been seeing the psychoanalyst twice a week." He took a sip of wine. Then he threw the remainder in the bartender's face.

The bartender wiped his face with a towel. "The doctor doesn't seem to be doing you any good," he sputtered.

"On the contrary," the man said, "He's done me a world of good."

"But you threw the wine in my face again!" the bartender exclaimed.

"Yes," the man said, "But it doesn't embarrass me anymore."

* * *

A worried Jewish mother takes her adolescent son to a psychoanalyst. After several visits the analyst asks to meet with the mother. "Your son has mentioned some things that frankly have me worried," says the analyst.

"Oh doctor," gushed the mother, "anything I can do to help my darling, I'll do."

"Well first," says the doctor, "I don't think it's a good idea to hold his hand when you walk together on the street. And second, I don't think it is healthy to take naps together on the same bed. Your son is developing what is called an Oedipus complex."

"Oedipus, Schmedipus," she replies, "just as long as he loves his mother."

* * *

After being introduced, the new member of the psychoanalytic interest group was asked if he would like to lie down and say a few words.

* * *

I had to go to analysis. They told me I had an unresolved Oedipus complex, which to them meant I want to sleep with my mother, which is preposterous. My father doesn't even want to sleep with my mother.

—*Dennis Wolfberg* (1992)

* * *

The young man said to his woman psychoanalyst: "I had the oddest dream last night. I dreamed you were my mother. I awoke and couldn't understand it. Why should I dream you were my mother?"

The analyst said, "Don't worry, you are experiencing what we call transference. What did you do after having the dream?"

"I had this appointment with you first thing in the morning, so I grabbed a cookie and a Coca Cola for breakfast and rushed over here," he replied.

The analyst frowned, "A cookie and a Coca Cola? That you call a breakfast?"

* * *

A man comes in to a psychoanalyst's office and lies down on the couch and starts to sleep. The irritated analyst asks, "What's your problem?"

The man says, "I don't have a room."

* * *

One analyst had two baskets on top of his desk. One was marked Outgoing; the other was marked Inhibited.

* * *

"Doctor, I have been in psychoanalysis for two years. Have you figured out what's wrong with me?"

"Yes, Mrs. Jones," responded the analyst, "you have a split personality."

"Baloney, Doc. I don't believe that, and neither do I."

* * *

A domineering wife was finally convinced by her husband that she needed treatment. After her first session she returned home, and her husband asked, "How did it go?"

"It was difficult," she said."It took me fifty minutes to convince the guy that his couch would look better against the far wall."

* * *

Two psychoanalysts are walking toward each other in the hall when the first analyst says good morning as they pass.

A few steps later, the second analyst looks back over her shoulder at the first and mutters, "I wonder what she meant by that?"

* * *

After she woke up, a woman told her husband, "I just dreamed you gave me a pearl necklace for our anniversary. What do you think the dream means?"

"You'll know tonight, darling," said the husband.

That evening the husband came home with a small wrapped package and gave it to his wife.

Delighted, she opened it up to find a book titled, *The Meaning of Dreams*.

Chapter Twelve

Urban Legends on the Couch: But I Read it in the Newspaper

The truth is rarely pure, and never simple.
  —Oscar Wilde (2003)

Urban legends are those highly captivating and plausible stories that have a moral, and friends swear they are true. These are the modern tales such as alligators in New York sewers, hairdos infested with spiders, and batter-fried rats in fast-food outlets.

Passed from person to person and embellished with local detail, they are eventually disseminated by the mass media. Inevitably, they are found in different versions through time and space. Such legends are usually introduced by, "I read it in the paper" or "I have a friend of a friend it happened to." When closely examined, however, these often-repeated-seldom-proven oral narratives, though told as true stories, are found to be mainly fiction.

The following mix of urban legends and psychiatric lore is about hospitals, professionals, and folks who use their help. They were told to me by a friend of a friend who knows the person it happened to—so, of course, they must be true.

Food for Thought

The wealthy owner of a large manufacturing company in the Midwest imported a French chef who went by the single name of Napoleon. His job was to be the major chef at the company's executive dining room. His roasts and sauces quickly became famous for miles around. One weekend, the president of a local university asked to borrow him to cook an important dinner for potential million-dollar donors.

As Napoleon prepared to leave his house, he couldn't find his knife satchel; so he wrapped the sharp blades in a piece of old newspaper and

153

got into his car. To his surprise, the car wouldn't start, so he went back into the house and called a local cab company. The dispatcher told him that all the cabs were spoken for, and he couldn't send one for at least an hour. Almost late for the event, Napoleon remembered that the bus went past his house and to the university on the other side of town.

He caught the bus in time; and breathing heavily from running, he shouted at the driver to "Step on zee gas, the prezident is waiting for me." The bus driver looked at Napoleon, and then looked at the carving knives wrapped in paper. He said, "You're the boss" and drove him straight to a psychiatric hospital

Seeing all the institutional type buildings, Napoleon was convinced that this was the university and began to unwrap his knives. To the guard at the front gate, he announced, "I'm Napoleon, take me to zee prezident."

Next thing he knew, he was being escorted to a holding cell by four large orderlies and then placed under lock and key.

University officials and his employer rescued Napoleon some eight hours later. It is said that he immediately returned to France where, "Zee peepuls are not zo cracee!"

—*Mikkelson and Mikkelson* (2006)

The Hook

There once was a couple who had been dating for a while who decided to "park" in the middle of a woods near a lake on a deserted Lover's Lane. While making out, their radio was on; and they listened to music from a popular local station. Then a news flash came on the radio that police were searching the outskirts of town for a man with a hook in place of his right hand. The man had just escaped from the psychiatric unit of a state prison—located near the Lover's Lane. He had been imprisoned for rape and murder.

Because he had a criminal history and was considered extremely dangerous, citizens were warned to lock their doors and to be especially cautious. The mood was broken, and the couple sat for a while with the girl becoming increasingly nervous. As a way of extending the intimacy of the evening, the boy pushed down the buttons on the inside of his door, automatically rolling up the windows and locking the car's doors. Feeling bold, he assured her they would be safe, and attempted to kiss her. Increasingly she became frantic, pushed him away, and insisted that they leave. "I'm scared," she cried. "Please take me back to town."

The young man argued with her, but finally gave in and drove back to her home. As he got out of the car and walked around to let his girlfriend out, he began to scream. Dangling from the rubber window molding on the passenger side window was a bloody hook.

Knit One, Purl Two

Bruno Bettelheim, the world famous Austrian child psychologist, taught at the University of Chicago. While there he gave a presentation on psychoanalysis to an undergraduate developmental psychology class in a large lecture hall. Shortly after he began, Bettelheim noticed an attractive young woman, sitting in the first row. Instead of taking notes however, she was concentrating on her knitting, and the sound of the needles interfered with his concentration.

Knitting during a lecture in an American university was seldom considered a problem. But, such behavior was *verboten* in a European classroom. Professor Bettelheim, every inch an authoritarian academic, was incensed and decided to teach this rude American a lesson in manners. Looking directly at her, and in his thick accent asked, "Young lady, do you know vat you are doing when you knit like that? You are masturbating."

The men in the class tittered while some of the women covered their mouths and giggled. Without looking up or dropping a stitch the young woman quietly replied, "Dr. Bettelheim, when I knit, I knit, and when I masturbate, I masturbate."

—*Maulding* (2002)

Give Him Some Air

A young medical social worker assigned to the intensive care unit of a general hospital was responsible for assisting patients and families with their psycho-social needs. A certain patient, an older gentleman and a particular favorite of the young lady, was connected to wires and tubes.

One morning as she was standing close to the patient's bed, his skin increasingly appeared ashen, and he struggled to breathe. Unable to speak, he gestured for a pen and pad on a table next to his bed. She passed them to him, and he awkwardly scribbled a note, and then pressed it into her hand. Fearful that he was dying, she stuffed the note into a pocket and reached over the bed triggering the emergency call system's "Code Blue" alert. Unfortunately, by the time help arrived the man was dead.

That night, extremely upset and sitting alone in her apartment, she remembered the note still in her pocket. She opened it and in horror read, "Please, you're standing on my air hose!"

Mental Patients Disappear

HARARE, Zimbabwe (04-04) After 20 mental patients disappeared from his bus, the driver replaced them with sane citizens and delivered them to a mental hospital.

The unidentified bus driver was transporting 20 mental patients from the capital city of Harare to Bulawayo Mental Hospital when he decided to stop for a few drinks at an illegal roadside liquor store. Upon his return, he was shocked to discover that all the mental patients had escaped.

Desperate for a solution, the driver stopped at the next bus stop and offered free bus rides to several people. He then delivered them to the mental hospital, warning the staff to be cautious, as they were easily excitable.

It took the medical personnel three days to uncover the foul play. The real mental patients are still at large.

This news story was allegedly published in the April 4, 1997 issue of South Africa's, Financial Mail. (Mikkelson and Mikkelson 2004)

Sigmund Freud

Sigmund Freud's supporters and detractors cannot agree whether the next three anecdotes are true and part of psychotherapy's oral tradition or merely humorous object lessons.

Have a Cigar Dr. Freud

In 1909, Sigmund Freud was invited to the United States to give a series of lectures at Clark University in Worcester, Massachusetts. His writings on psychoanalysis preceded him and terms such as "libido," "penis envy," and the "unconscious" had crept into the language. Freud's books were popular, and people who had the money to afford it were asking to be "analyzed."

Something else preceded Freud—the persistent rumor that he was addicted to the countless cigars he smoked each day. One evening Freud gave a lecture to a distinguished and highly trained audience. The topic was psychosexual development and the significance of the oral, anal, and phallic stage in a person's development.

At the end of the lecture a mischievous fellow, who had heard the cigar rumor, decided to put Freud on the spot. "Dr. Freud," he said, "You have spoken about oral fixation and the unconscious meaning of phallic symbols. What is the psychoanalytic significance of smoking a cigar?"

Freud hesitated a second and then without embarrassment smiled and answered, "Sir, sometimes a cigar is just a cigar."

Treatment by the Numbers

Another legend about Freud takes place in rural Massachusetts where he was invited by a superintendent to visit a mental institution located on the outskirts of town. After touring the hospital facilities and lunching with the staff physicians, he boarded the bus to return home. As he sat down, a hospital staff member brought in some patients who were going on a field trip to the city. When they were in their seats the staff person began to count, "One, two, three, four, five, six." When he got to Freud he asked, "Who are you?"

Freud said, "I'm Sigmund Freud."

The staff member went on, "Seven, eight, nine..."

The Great Depression

A certain man found himself in a serious state of depression. Since he was in Vienna at the time, he decided he would make an appointment with a young doctor named Sigmund Freud, about whom people were saying good things.

He obtained an appointment and explained his problem. Freud listened patiently and said, "My friend, this is not something that can be alleviated in a short conversation or even in a few days. You will have to undergo a long course of treatment—if you can find someone who is capable of giving it to you."

Dr. Freud continued, "Meanwhile, the great clown Grimaldi is in town. I have seen him, and I assure you that no one can watch him without laughing uproariously. Why not go to see Grimaldi and get at least a few hours of comfort, and, perhaps, some joy?"

"That is impossible, Dr. Freud," said the man.

"How so?" asked the doctor.

"Because I am the great clown Grimaldi," he replied.

Crazy Doesn't Mean Stupid

A university professor was driving by a psychiatric hospital in his large Buick when a tire went flat. He pulled off the road, jacked up his car, and struggled to loosen the lug nuts. Not accustomed to changing tires, he awkwardly removed all five lug nuts and put them in the hub cap. Just as he was getting ready to put on the spare, a speeding car came too close, hit the hub cap, and threw the lug nuts all over a 10-acre field. The professor was stumped about what to do.

In the meantime, one of the institutionalized patients had been watching and he called out, "Why don't you take one nut from each of the other wheels and put them on the new tire. It'll work until you get to a garage."

The professor was impressed by the idea and did what the man suggested. Then he thanked him and said, "Why are you in there? You're not crazy."

"Oh, I'm mentally ill all right," the patient said, "I'm just not stupid."

Grand Delusions

In the day room of a state hospital, a psychiatric nurse was talking to a patient about his delusions. He was convinced that he was Napoleon, and the nurse was bound and determined to convince him he wasn't.

Nurse: You are not Napoleon.

Patient: Yes, I am.

Nurse: Wrong. Your name is Frank Wilson

Patient: You're wrong. It's Napoleon.

Nurse: How long have you been Napoleon?

Patient: All my life.

Nurse: What are your parent's names?

Patient: Mr. and Mrs. Napoleon, and they live in France.

Nurse: No, their names are Mr. and Mrs. Wilson, and they live in New Jersey.

After twenty minutes of this no-win dialogue, the nurse was totally frustrated and the patient was upset. But, despite feeling thwarted, she wasn't willing to admit defeat.

Nurse: (angrily) Who told you you're Napoleon?

Patient: (loudly) God told me I'm Napoleon!

From a patient sitting in a rocking chair in the corner came: I did not tell you you're Napoleon!

Passive Aggressive Revenge

A lady in England returned home unexpectedly from a marital counseling session only to hear noises upstairs in her bedroom. She slowly climbed the stairs, fearful that robbers had broken in and were stealing her jewelry. Nearing the second floor, she recognized her husband's voice and the amorous sounds of a woman. Clearly they were having a most creative and enjoyable time on the couple's bed. Making no noise, she returned to the main floor, let herself out of the house, and returned home at the expected time.

That evening the wife cooked a fine dinner, taking care to grind up some sleeping-pills and include them in the mashed potatoes—her husband's favorite dish. Pleading exhaustion, the husband retired early to bed. Shortly after he was asleep she stripped him of his pajamas and stuck his hand to his penis with Super Glue.

Doctors and nurses at the local hospital had the unenviable task of separating manual and genital flesh from their tangle. More challenging was improvising an arrangement to enable the patient to urinate.

A Queen You Say

The popular and democratic Elizabeth, Queen of the Belgians, visited the United States after World War I. She wanted to show her appreciation for the assistance the American people had given the Belgians during the war. Knowing little about the various states, nor the American people, she was committed to learning as much as she could during her visit. Of special interest was her curiosity about medical care, particularly hospital treatment of the mentally ill. To this end, she read everything she could about American hospitals, doctors, and the latest advances in psychiatric medicine.

One day, the Queen went unheralded, unaccompanied, and unannounced to the Henry Phipps Psychiatric Clinic of Johns Hopkins Hospital in Baltimore. The Queen inquired where she might find Doctor Adolf Myer, the famous director of this clinic. When she located the doctor, the Queen introduced herself as the Queen of the Belgians.

And, always the gentleman, the doctor bowed, smiled gently, and then soothingly replied, "That's very interesting. Tell me, how long have you thought so?"

—*Worthington* (Winter 2008)

Go Eat Worms

Because of his refusal to eat, a frantic mother took her little son to an internationally known child guidance clinic in Boston. On the staff was a psychiatrist famous for his work with children who had eating disorders. After a physical evaluation, which provided no clues, the doctor offered the boy every conceivable goody, but to no avail. Finally he said, "What would you like to eat?" "Worms," was the calm reply.

Not to be outdone, the doctor sent his nurse out for a plate full of the wrigglers. "Here," he barked to the boy. "I want them fried," came the answer.

The nurse took them into the clinic's kitchen, fried them, and returned with the plate.

"I only want one," said the food-hater.

The doctor got rid of all but one. "Now," he exploded "eat!" The boy protested, "You eat half."

The doctor was not going to be manipulated. He ate half of the worm, and then dangled the remaining half in the little fellow's face. The boy burst into tears.

"What's the matter now?" yelled the infuriated doctor. "You ate my half," the little boy wailed.

Just a Reminder

When Franklin Roosevelt was governor of New York State, his wife Eleanor arrived one day unannounced to inspect a state mental hospital. A distinguished-looking man recognized her when she came to the entrance and at once offered his services as a guide on her tour.

In the course of several hours of careful inspection, Mrs. Roosevelt became increasingly impressed by the knowledge and intelligence her guide possessed, his gentle manners, and his obvious good breeding. In taking her leave, she thanked him and expressed her belief that the hospital was in good hands.

"Oh, I'm not a staff member here, I'm a patient," explained her guide. He told her how he had been unjustly committed by greedy members of his family who had designs on his personal fortune and a greater fortune he was soon to inherit. His detailed and reasonable account of the conspiracy that had resulted in his commitment caused Mrs. Roosevelt to promise to have the governor make an immediate investigation and correct whatever injustice had been done. The patient thanked her gravely for her kindness.

As she turned to go down the steps, a vigorous kick in the posterior caused Mrs. Roosevelt to stumble and nearly fall down the stairs. Gasping with shocked indignation, she demanded, "Why did you do that? You might have hurt me seriously."

The patient smiled gently. "I didn't want to hurt you. I did it so you would not forget to tell the governor about my case."

—*Robert Wood* (1967)

Just Hanging Around

A 20-year-old inmate at a county jail planned a circuitous route to freedom. His plan, which seemed to make sense at the time, was to pretend he was mentally ill, in order that the jail staff would transfer him to a nearby minimum-security mental health facility. Once there, he would engineer a more permanent escape back into the community.

His plan seemed simple enough. He would hang himself with a bed sheet. Once unconscious, his cell mates would cut him down and alert the jail guards, who would certainly send him to the psychiatric unit.

Unfortunately, only half of the plan worked. He tore the sheet into strips, made a semblance of a rope, hooked it to window bars, knotted a loop around his neck—and then strangled himself. By the time he was cut down, he was quite dead. His wish to leave jail, however, was fulfilled the following day when his body was removed, taken to a near-by hospital for an autopsy, and subsequently buried.

This legend is based on an occurrence that happened in Stephens Point, Wisconsin.

—Northcutt (2000)

FBI Get Their Pizza

In the 1990's the FBI assisted the Department of Health and Human Services in investigating health care fraud. A medical corporation that operated several psychiatric hospitals in the United States had come under suspicion, and coordinated raids on the hospitals took place on the same day. The bulk of the records seized in one of the hospitals meant that the investigation would require FBI staff to work all day and late into the night. After many hours, the agent in charge decided to order pizza from a local pizza shop. The following phone conversation is reconstructed from the memories of the agents.

Agent: That's right, I'm an FBI agent.

Pizza Man: You're an FBI Agent?

Agent: That's right, just about everyone here is.

Pizza Man: And you're at the psychiatric hospital?

Agent: That's correct. And make sure you don't go through the front doors. We have the doors locked. You'll have to go around to the back to the service entrance to deliver the pizzas.

Pizza Man: You say you're all FBI agents?

Agent: That's right. How soon can you have them here?

Pizza Man: And you're over at the hospital?

Agent: That's right. How soon can you have them here?

Pizza Man: And everyone at the hospital is an FBI agent?

Agent: That's right. We've been here all day, and we're starving.

Pizza man: How are you going to pay for this?

Agent: I have my checkbook right here.

Pizza Man: And you are all FBI agents?

Agent: That's right. Everyone here is an FBI agent. Can you remember to bring the pizzas and sodas to the service entrance in the rear? We have the front doors locked.

Pizza Man: I don't think so. (Click)

And, yes, the FBI agents did get their pizzas, but had to go to the pizza shop and pick them up.

According to researchers who study urban legends, there is truth to this tale. Reportedly it took place at Southwood Psychiatric Hospital in Chula Vista, CA in 1993 (Mikkelson and Mikkelson 2004).

Training the Professor

There is the story about a graduate course on behaviorism in which the students decided to apply the power of positive reinforcement. The students agreed that when the professor stood near the waste paper basket in the front corner of the classroom they would pay close attention, nod, and take copious notes. When he wandered to another part of the classroom they fidgeted, yawned, and shuffled papers. The reinforcement worked. By the end of two weeks, the professor delivered his whole lecture in the corner of the room next to the waste basket. Experiencing success they decided to bump the experiment up a notch. Every session, a student arrived early to class and turned over the waste basket. Now, when he lectured they would only pay attention if he stood in the corner with one foot on the basket. The class modified the professor's behavior to the point that when he entered the classroom he would pick up the basket, carry it to the same spot at the front of the room, turn it over, climb on top of it—and then begin his lecture.

A Monkey's Uncle

Psychologists at a mid-western primate language institute were teaching a group of chimpanzees to communicate using symbols and non-verbal cues. One particular monkey was truly exceptional. Not only could he understand language, he could read. One day the monkey escaped from its trainers, dashed out of the laboratory and raced through the campus. Evading capture, he ran first into a dormitory, then the student union and the administration building with psychology faculty, campus police, plus curious students in pursuit.

Frightened, the errant savant entered the front door of the library and hurdled down the stairs to the basement stacks, filled with hundreds of thousands of books. Doors were quickly locked and searchers began to systematically seek out the chimpanzee. After about an hour, he was discovered in a corner of the stacks, sitting on a pile of manuscripts with a book in each hand. Appearing puzzled, the artful dodger stared back and forth, first at the book in his right hand, then the book in his left hand.

Fearful that they would spook the frightened monkey, one of the behaviorists cautiously began to communicate with him using hand signals. After a few minutes another searcher asked what the monkey was reading.

"Well," whispered the trainer, "in his right hand is the *Holy Bible* and in his left hand, Darwin's *Origins of the Species*."

"So why does he looks so frustrated?" asked another.

"If I understand him," said the trainer, "he's confused. He can't figure out whether he's his brother's-keeper or he's his keeper's-brother."

Should I Tell My Bride-to-Be?

Dear Ann Landers:

I'm writing you for advice, and hope you can help me.

First, I'm a sailor in the United States Navy, and I also have a cousin who is a social worker. My father has epilepsy and my mother has syphilis, so neither of them are employed. They are dependent on my two sisters who are prostitutes in Cleveland, because my only brother is serving a life term in prison for sodomy and murder. He was imprisoned a year before my uncle was hospitalized for attempting to kill the president.

I am in love with a streetwalker who operates near our base. She knows nothing of my background but says that she loves me. It's our hope to get married as soon as she settles her bigamy case which is now in court. When I get out of the Navy we intend to move to Pittsburgh and open up a small business.

*My problem is this. In view of the fact that I plan to make
this girl my wife and bring her into my family, should I or
shouldn't I tell her about my cousin who is a social worker?*

*Versions of this letter were reportedly published in Ann Landers and
"Dear Abby" advice columns.*

Seeing is Believing

A psychiatrist was asked to do an evaluation on a teenage boy,
hospitalized the night before because of anxiety and depression. As he
entered the hospital room, the boy was lying in bed. His mother was
sitting next to him knitting. After introducing himself to the mother
and the teenager, he asked the reason for the hospitalization. The
words where no more out off his mouth before the boy began to
scream, "I can't see, I can't see!"

"Amazing," thought the psychiatrist, "this is one of the most
curious examples of hysterical blindness I've ever seen."

"This must be very difficult for you," he said, using his most I feel
your pain empathy. "How long has this been going on?"

"Ever since you stepped in front of the television," said the mother
without looking up.

A Half Nelson

According to lore, a new patient at London's Bethlem Royal Hospital—often called "Bedlam"—announced that he was Lord Nelson.
Interestingly, the institution already had a "Lord Nelson." The head
physician decided the men should meet, hoping that the similarity of
their delusions might prompt an adjustment leading to their cures.

The plan was met with trepidation by the staff who asked, "What if
the two men react violently to one another?" It was agreed that they
were taking a risk but the decision was made to try it. That evening
the men were introduced and left alone to get to know each other.

The following morning, the doctor met with his new patient and
was surprised when he was told, "Doctor, I've been suffering from
delusions of grandeur. I know now that I'm not Lord Nelson."

"That's wonderful," said the doctor.

"Yes," said the patient, smiling confidently. "I'm Lady Nelson."

Chapter Thirteen

Shrink, Shrank, Shrunk: Coming to Terms

*All the world is queer save me and thee; and sometimes I
think thee is a little queer.*
> —attributed to a Quaker speaking to his wife (Bartlett, 1992)

Our language reveals lots about who we are and the ways in which we view folks who are different from us. According to the *Thesaurus*, there are dozens of euphemisms for being normal, and hundreds of expressions—and certainly much more colorful ones—for those we judge to be eccentric or a bit peculiar. Take me for example. I'm reasonable, lucid, sensible, well-grounded, and misunderstood. I have all my marbles. Furthermore, I am level-headed, all there, of sound mind; and I exhibit good judgment.

You, on the other hand, are as crazy as a bedbug (or bat, beetle, barn owl, coot, loon, and June-Bug-in-May), and have bats in your belfry. You're also mad as a hatter (or March hare and monkey on a trike), psycho, nutty as a fruit cake, a wack-job, bonkers, screwy, cracked, cuckoo, berserk, and just plain nuts.

The following dictionary, albeit a bit convoluted, provides a fresh approach to psychotherapy and the human condition.

A

Absurdity: Statement or belief manifestly inconsistent with one's own opinion.

Adolescence: The stage between puberty and adultery.

Adult: Someone who has stopped growing at both ends and started growing in the middle.

Adultery: Two wrong people doing the right thing.

Advice: Approval sought for doing something one has decided to do.

Air Head: What a woman intentionally becomes when pulled over by a traffic cop.

Alter Ego: Unrealistic belief you can change the person you are marrying.

Altered Ego: Changes that occurs in newlyweds two hours after the wedding.

Alcoholic: Someone you don't like who drinks as much as you do.

Alimony: A contraction for "all my money."

Ambivalence: Seeing your mother-in-law backing off a cliff in your new car.

Amnesia: Nature's way of saying, "Forget it!"

Angoraphobia: A persistent and unreasonable fear of sweaters.

Atrophy: What you get for winning the Boston Marathon.

B

Behaviorism: The art of pulling habits out of rats.

Bigamist: Someone with one marriage too many.

Bigamy: When two rites make a wrong.

Born-again Christian: A person benefiting from a faith lift.

Braggart: Someone who always puts his feats in his mouth.

Bucolic Plague: A case load consisting of impoverished rural families.

Bulldozing: Falling asleep during a statistics lecture.

C

Chastity: Most unnatural of sexual perversions.

Cherpies: A tweatable STD transmitted by birds.

Child Psychology: What parents use when letting their children have their own way.

Child Therapist: A person who used to think she liked children.

Childish Behavior: Anyone who is doing what we only wish we could still do.

Children: Creatures who disgrace you by exhibiting in public the example you set for them at home.

Claustrophobia: Fear of Santa.

Clinical Notes: Documents kept for thirty years, then thrown away the day you need them.

College Professor: Someone who talks in other people's sleep.

Committee: Group that keeps the minutes but loses hours.

Confidence: That quiet assured feeling you have before you fall flat on your face.

Conscience: Something that feels terrible when everything else feels swell.

Consultant: An ordinary person with a briefcase, more than 50 miles from home.

Consultation: Medical term that means share the wealth.

Coward: One who in a perilous emergency thinks with his legs.

Crisis-du-Jour: Acute craziness perpetuated by one's daily life.

Crock Pot: Individual suffering from half-cooked and half-baked ideas.

Cynic: A man who, when he smells flowers, looks around for the coffin.

Cynicism: The intellectual cripple's substitute for intelligence.

D

Death: Nature's way of telling you to slow down.

Demean: Procedure that reduces nastiness in individuals.

Denial: A river in Egypt.

Depressed: Someone who sees the world as it really is.

Depression: Anger without enthusiasm.

Derange: Where the buffalo roam.

Diplomat: A person who praises marriage but remains single.

Divorce: Past tense of marriage.

E

Edifice Complex: A psychotherapist more interested in his office space than his clients' well-being.

Egotism: Self-intoxication.

Egotist: A person who is always me-deep in conversation.

Enthusiasm: Hope with a tin can tied to its tail.

Experience: The name men give to their mistakes.

Expert: One who has a good reason for guessing wrong.

F

Fair Divorce: When each party thinks he or she got the best deal.

Fanatic: One who will stick to his guns whether they are loaded or not.

Fate: Confusion of bad management and destiny.

Feedback: The result when a baby doesn't appreciate the strained carrots.

Flattery: An insult in gift wrapping.

Freudian-slip: When you say one thing but mean your mother.

Freudian Virus: Infection causing one's personal computer to become obsessed with its own mother-board.

Frustration: Trying to find your glasses without your glasses.

Funeral Eulogy: A belated plea for the defense delivered after all the evidence is in.

G

Genital: Non-Jewish person.

Genius: Someone who is a crackpot until he hits the jackpot.

Geriatrics: The science that attempts to solve the age-old problem of old age.

Groundless Apprehension: That uneasy feeling right after the plane takes off.

Group Therapy: A method based on the theory that a cure will come if a group of similarly afflicted people are rude enough to each other.

Guilt: The gift that goes on giving.

H

Hangover: The wrath of grapes.

Happiness: An agreeable sensation arising from contemplating the misery of others.

Hate Organizations: Sour groups.

Headache: Aspirin deficiency.

Hemorrhoidic Myopia: A crappy outlook on life.

Heredity: What a man believes in until his son makes a fool of himself.

High Risk: Potential problems when a psychotherapist counsels a malpractice attorney.

Hindsight: What one experiences from changing too many diapers.

Hope: Disappointment deferred.

Hospital: A place where people who run down wind up.

Humor: A smoke screen that keeps you from being blinded by the truth.

Hypochondria: Person suffering from wanting to have his ache and treat it too.

Hypochondriacs: People who enjoy bad health.

Hypocrite: A person who writes a book in praise of atheism, and prays for it to be a best seller.

I

Ill-literate: Someone who becomes anxious from reading a book on psychopathology.

Impotent: Distinguished and well known.

Incongruous: A place where laws are made.

Inpatient: Someone who is tired of waiting.

Insanity: Grounds for divorce in some states; grounds for marriage in all.

Insurance: Something costing thousands of dollars so that when you are dead you will have nothing to worry about.

Intelligent Tests: Hocus pocus used by psychologists to prove that they are brilliant and their patients are stupid.

Intuition: Instinct that tells a woman she is right, whether she is or not.

Invoice: A conscience doing its job.

J

Jealous: Moral indignation with a halo.

Jealousy: An emotional case of poison envy.

Juvenile Delinquent: Result of parents trying to train children without starting at the bottom.

L

Life: A hereditary disease.

Listening: Silent flattery.

Love: Insanity with a collaborator.

Lust-less: Sensuality, licentiousness, wantonness, and passion—all in short supply.

M

Malingering: Reluctance to leave one's mother.

Mandate: Two gay men out for dinner and a movie.

Manic Depressive: Easy glum, easy glow.

MAO Inhibitors: A class of antidepressants that helps to control Chinese communists.

Marriage: (1) A union that defies management. (2) A knot tied by a minister and untied by a lawyer.

Martyr: Someone who has to live with a saint.

Masturbation: Preferred mode of sexual gratification for those who prefer the imaginary to the real.

Maternal Combustion: Mother's response to her children after spending two rainy days together in a tent.

Matrimony: Splice of life.

Mental Block: Street where several therapists live.

Mentally Incontinent: An overactive mind resulting in an urgency to leak thoughts.

Middle-Age: Time of life when the most fun you have is talking about the fun you use to have.

Middle-Aged: What old people insist on calling themselves.

Morality: The attitude you adopt for people whom you personally dislike.

Morbid: A higher bid.

N

Nagging: Repetition of impalpable truths.

Narcissism: Individuals of low taste more interested in themselves than in you.

Narcissistic: Person whose eyes become glazed when conversation wanders away from them.

Near-life Experience: Growth that occurs when one's denial no longer works.

Neurotic: A person who has discovered the secret of perpetual emotions.

Nymphomaniac: Woman obsessed with sex as much as the average man.

O

Optimist: A person who falls off the Empire State Building and, as he passes the 75th floor yells, "I'm all right."

Orgasm: Grand finale.

Outpatient: Someone who faints in the therapist's office.

P

Paradox: Two psychiatrists.

Paralyze: Couple of lies.

Pathological: A reasonable way to go.

Patience: The practice of concealing your impatience.

Perfectionist: Someone who takes infinite pains ... then gives them to everyone else.

Perversion: Sexual practice disproved by the speaker.

Pessimist: A person who won't hang his stocking from the mantle for fear Santa Claus will steal it.

Post-traumatic Dress Syndrome: Two women at a party, wearing the same dress.

Poverty: A state of mind often induced by a neighbor's new car.

Praise: Letting off esteem.

Prejudice: Being positive about something negative.

Procrastination: The art of keeping up with yesterday.

Procrastinator: One who puts off until tomorrow things he already put off until today.

Professor: A person whose job it is to tell students how to solve the problems of life that they have tried to avoid by becoming an academic.

Projective Tests: Hocus-pocus used by psychologists to prove they are normal and their clients are crazy.

Prude: Someone who wants their conscience to be your guide.

Psychiatrist's Couch: Bunk bed.

Psycho-ceramics: Treatment of choice for crack pots.

Psychology: The science that tells you what you already know in words you can't understand.

Psycho-social history: Study of a person's unhappiness.

R

Realist: Person who is preparing to do something he is secretly ashamed of.

Repartee: What a person thinks after he becomes a departee.

Resolve: That admirable quality in ourselves that is detestable stubbornness in others.

Revenge: Sweetest word in the English language.

S

Sadist: A person who is kind to a masochist.

Saints: Those honored in heaven but considered hell on earth.

Seasoning Affective Disorder: A low-level of emotional spice in one's life.

Secret: Something you tell to one person at a time.

Self-centered: Someone better looking than you.

Self-defeating Prophecy: Putting away money for an emergency.

Self-respect: The secure feeling that no one, as yet, is suspicious.

Sense of Humor: Laughing at an event that would make you angry if it happened to you.

Sex: An emotion in motion.

Sex Maniac: Husband who wants more children than his wife does.

Show-off: A child who is more talented than yours.

Shrink: A therapist who reduces patients' illusions, delusions, and net worth.

Shrink Rap: A discussion group for therapists.

Siblings: Children of the same parents, each of whom is perfectly sane until they get together.

Silence: Only thing that cannot be misquoted.

Sociology: The study of people who do not need to be studied by people who do.

Specialist: A generalist with a small practice and a large home.

Statistician: Someone who does not have the personality to be an accountant.

Statistics: Art of never having to say you are wrong.

Stress: The confusion created when one's mind overrides the body's desire to choke the hell out of some dumb twit who desperately needs it.

Stressed: When you wake up screaming and realize you haven't fallen asleep yet.

Suicide: A permanent solution to a temporary problem.

Syntax: What the compiler of a treasury like this ought to be required to pay his readers.

T

Tact: Changing the subject without changing your mind.

Tears: Remorse code.

Teenagers: God's punishment for having sex.

Tension: The price one pays for being a race horse instead of a plow horse.

Terminal Illness: Experiencing acute anxiety at the airport.

Theory: An educated hunch.

Therapeuticus interruptus: Therapy abruptly terminated when insurance company refuses to pay benefits.

Tolerance: Letting other people find happiness in their way instead of yours.

Transvestite: Someone who eats, drinks, and be Mary.

Tricycleics: Antidepressants for children.

V

Vanity: Gift wrapping yourself.

Variance: What any two statisticians are at.

Virginity: A big issue about a little tissue.

Vu déjà: Feeling you have never been here before.

W

Wedding: Necessary formality before securing a divorce.

Well-Adjusted: Making the same mistake over and over and over without getting upset.

Wife: A man's side kicker.

Will Power: Looking into the eyes of a topless waitress.

Worry: Interest paid on trouble before it falls due.

Y

Yawn: An honest opinion openly expressed.

References

Abel, Milt. "Mental Health Jokes." *www.comedycentraljokes.com*. 2009. (accessed March 02, 2009).

Annie Hall. Directed by Woody Allen. Performed by Woody Allen. 1997.

Ayres, Alex. *Wit and Wisdom of Mark Twain*. New York: Harper & Row, 1987.

Bamford, Maria. "Mental Health Jokes." *www.comedycentraljokes.com*. 2009. (accessed March 02, 2009).

Bartlett, John. *Bartlett's Familiar Quotations: A Collection of Passages*. Boston: Little Brown,1992.

Berle, Milton. *Milton Berle's Private Joke File*. New York: Three Rivers Press, 1989.

Braverman, Shirley J. "Final Exams." *American Journal of Nursing*, June 1980: Vol.80, no. 6, 1234.

Brown, Rita Mae. *Yale Book of Quotations*. Fred Shapiro, editor. New Haven: Yale University Press, 2006.

Crisp, Quentin. *The Naked Public Servant*. London: Penguin Press, 1968.

Dali, Salvadore. *Columbia Dictionary of Familiar and Famous Quotations*. [from *Diary of a Genius*, May 1952] New York: Columbia University Press, 1966.

Davis, DelRay. "Mental Health Jokes." *www.comedycentraljokes.com*. 2009. (accessed March 02, 2009).

DeVries, Peter. *Portable Curmudgeon*, by Jon Winokur. New York: New American Library, 1987.

Financial Mail. "Mental Patients Disappear." Harare Zimbabwe. April 4, 1997.

Galifanakis, Zack. "Mental Health Jokes." *comedycentraljokes.com*. 2009. (accessed March 02, 2009).

Goldwyn, Samuel. *The Moguls* by Norman Zierold. New York: Coward-McCann, 1969.

Katz, Jonathon. "Mental Health Jokes." *www.comedycentraljokes.com*. 2009. (accessed March 02, 2009).

King, Storm. *www.stormpsych@charter.net*. (accessed March 01, 2007).

Levant, Oscar. From *Encyclopedia Neurotica* by Jon Winokur. New York: St. Martin's Press, 2005.

Levenson, Sam. *You can say that again, Sam: The choice wisdom of Sam Levenson*. Boston: G.K. Hall, 1979.

Maron, Mark. "Mental Health Jokes." *www.comedycentraljokes.* (accessed March 02, 2009).

Maulding, Joseph. "Speak Memory, or Goodbye Columbus." *Journal of Personality Assessment,* 2002: 4-30.

McGrew, Steve. "Mental Health Jokes." *www.comedycentraljokes.com.* 2009. (accessed March 02, 2009).

Menninger, Karl. *Encyclopedia Neurotica* by Jon Winokur, 152. New York: St. Martin's Press, 2005.

Mikkelson, Barbara, and Mikkelson, David. *www.snopes.com/medicine/ asylum/fbipizza.asp.* December 31, 2004. (accessed September 13, 2006).

Mindess, Harvey. "The Use and Abuse of Humor in Psychotherapy," in *Humor and Laughter: Theory, Research and Applications* by Antony Chapman and Hugh Foot (337), Hoboken NJ: John Wiley and Sons, 1976.

Nickman, Bob. "Mental Health Jokes." *www.comedycentraljokes.com.* 2009. (accessed March 02, 2009).

Northcutt, Wendy. *The Darwin Awards: Evolution in Action*. New York: Dutton, 2000.

Owen, Guy. *Comedy Comes Clean* by Adam Christing, New York: Crown Trade Paperback, 1996.

Parker, Dorothy. "Resume." *Poems of Dorothy Parker*. New York: Boni & Liveright, 1926.

Quinn, Colin. "Mental Health Jokes." *www.comedycentraljokes.com.* 2009. (accessed March 02, 2009).

Rea, Caroline. "Mental Health Jokes." *www.comedycentraljokes.com.* 2009. (accessed March 02, 2009).

Rosenberg, Leo. *www.advocate.org.* Fall, #24, 2003. (accessed March 02, 2009).

Schulz, Charles. *You Don't Look 35 Charlie Brown*. New York: Holt, Rinehart and Winston, 1985.

Shakes, Ronnie. *Comedy Quote Dictionary* by Ron Smith. New York: Doubleday, 1992.

Shaw, George Bernard. *Encarta Book of Quotations*, Bill Swanson, editor. New York: St. Martin's Press, 2000.

Szasz, Thomas. *The Second Sin*. Garden City: Anchor Press, 1973.

White, Chris. *www.topfive.com*. (accessed March 23, 2007).

Wilde, Oscar. *The Oxford Dictionary of Literary Quotations*. Peter Kemp, editor. [From *The Importance of Being Earnest*] Oxford: Oxford University Press, 2003.

Wilmot, John, Earl of Rochester. *The Concise Columbia Dictionary of Quotations*. Robert Andrews, editor. New York: Columbia University Press, 1989.

Wolfberg, Dennis. *Comedy Quote Dictionary*. New York: Doubleday, 1992.

Wood, Robert. *Modern Handbook of Humor*. New York: McGraw Hill, 1967.

Worthington, Janet Farrar. "When Psychiatry was Young." *Hopkins*, Winter 2008: 180.

Wright, Steve. "Steve Wright's Humor." *www.fortogden.com*. (accessed March 02, 2009).

CPSIA information can be obtained
at www.ICGtesting.com
Printed in the USA
BVHW02s0037271217
503705BV00007B/111/P

9 781596 637351